THE GAZEBO

THE GAZEBO

Emily Grayson

DOUBLEDAY DIRECT LARGE PRINT EDITION

William Morrow and Company, Inc.
New York

This Large Print Edition, prepared especially for Doubleday Direct, Inc., contains the complete unabridged text of the original Publisher's Edition.

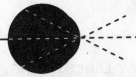

**This Large Print Book carries the
Seal of Approval of N.A.V.H.**

TO MY CHILDREN

With many thanks to
Lisa Queen and Claire Wachtel
for all their help and encouragement

THE GAZEBO

CHAPTER ONE

The man with the silver hair had been standing in the doorway even before she knew he was there. How long, she couldn't say. Abby just looked up, and there he was, not knocking. He hadn't asked for her at the front desk, or someone would have called her. He hadn't asked for directions down the hall to her office, or someone would have accompanied him. Instead, he'd simply found her, as if he knew his way around the place, and then he stood there, as if he were willing to wait forever.

"Yes?" she said to him, bending back to the work on her desk.

"Forgive the interruption," the man said. "But I have something that may interest you."

"I'm sorry. I'm very busy." Abby kept reading the printout of a page proof and entering her corrections into the computer on the edge of her desk. She didn't want to appear impolite, but this was a newspaper; there were deadlines. Show up unannounced in the editor's office and you couldn't expect her undivided attention. "So," she said, checking, typing, "can this wait?"

"I'm afraid not," he said.

She glanced up. The man in her doorway was wearing a light linen jacket and setting a very worn but well-made briefcase down on the floor. He didn't seem to be from around here, yet she couldn't be sure. Abby hesitated, then returned to her work.

"This will take only a minute," he went on. "You *are* Abby Reston, aren't you?"

She nodded, not looking up.

"I have a story I'd like you to know about," he said. "Something you might be interested in printing in the *Ledger*. A human interest story, I guess."

It was just as she'd thought. The *Ledger* was an institution of sorts in these parts, dat-

ing back to the middle of the previous century, and since she'd taken over as editor
six months earlier Abby had often found
herself on the receiving end of a faithful
reader's suggestion for a "wonderful" article: missing wedding rings, the death of a
beloved schnauzer, feuds between neighbors. Usually, what someone thought was
perfect for a newspaper turned out to be too
personal, too particular, or simply not interesting enough. "You should talk to one of
our reporters," Abby told him. "I can put you
in touch with—"

"No," the man said, interrupting.

Abby glanced up again.

"It's a story that needs to be written by
someone who can really write. I think this
story is for you to write," he continued.
"Maybe I could tell it to you, and then you
can decide."

She looked at the computer screen, its
cursor blinking impatiently, then at the unmoving man in the doorway. "If you can say
what it's about in a sentence or two," she
said.

The man nodded. "It's a love story," he
said.

"Well, we could use more of those in the

world," said Abby. She leaned back in her chair, its wooden joints heaving slightly.

"It's about myself," he continued. "I'm sorry, I haven't even given you my name. It's Martin Rayfiel."

He seemed to be studying her for a response. She shook her head slightly, gave a mild shrug. "Should I know you?"

He smiled, almost to himself. "Not really," he said. "It's just that the name sometimes used to get a reaction around here." Then he drew himself straight, getting down to business. "I'll make this quick." He took a breath and began. "Every year at dusk on May twenty-seventh, I meet the woman I love in the gazebo in the town square. It's the only time we have a chance to be together." He inclined his chin in the direction of Abby's screen window. She turned in her chair to follow his gaze across the street to the town square, and across the town square to the gazebo, where a small boy was sitting with his mother, unhappily submitting to her efforts to clean his face with a wet wipe.

"Once a year," she said, and he nodded. Not a wife, then, Abby thought. A lover? But then why tell Abby? And why ask Abby to tell the world—or Longwood Falls, anyway? He'd succeeded in beginning to arouse her curiosity, but that was nothing, Abby knew; it was her job to be curious. The question was whether anyone else would care about this apparently private annual event. Abby peered down at the day-at-a-glance calendar on her desk. "Tomorrow's the twenty-seventh," she said to him.

He nodded again. "Claire and I have been meeting on May twenty-seventh at the gazebo for quite some time. Actually, we've been doing it for fifty years. And we never missed a year."

Fifty years. Abby had only just turned thirty-five; she could barely imagine being alive for such a long time, let alone having loved someone for so long. She looked again at this man, closely, as if for the first time. Martin Rayfiel was not young, but his appearance was striking, and young in its own way. His hair was slightly long and shot through with silver, brushed back off his face as though with an impatient hand. He was probably in his late sixties, around the age her father would have been, she realized, and then when she tried to picture Martin Rayfiel as a much younger man, his silver hair an uninterrupted black, his long features unlined, his slender hands tracing the face of a young woman—when she tried to picture him as a young man just falling in love— it was her father's face that came to mind. And then it wasn't, because Abby couldn't imagine her father, however much he'd loved her mother up to the moment of his death seven months earlier, in the grip of something approximating passion.

"Excuse me? Abby?" It was Kim, the newspaper's combination classified ad saleswoman and receptionist, suddenly hovering behind Martin Rayfiel in the office doorway. She was a small, overly caffeinated young woman in a pink headband, and she was shifting from foot to foot. Martin stepped aside, and Kim said, "I have to get those forms in by this afternoon?"

At the moment, Abby couldn't remember what forms Kim was talking about, but she quickly apologized and told Kim that of course she'd be right with her. "I'm sorry," Abby said to Martin. "I'd like to hear the rest, but . . ." and she gestured toward Kim, her computer, the obediently waiting cursor.

"That's all right," Martin Rayfiel said softly. "We'll just chalk it up to bad timing on my part." This, too, seemed to amuse him in some private way. "Well, thank you. I tried anyway. You've been very gracious, and I appreciate it." He bowed his head once, and then he picked up his briefcase and walked out the door, slipping away as quietly as he had come.

Abby wanted to call out to him, but what would she say? Even if she could find the time to hear the rest of his story, she still didn't know whether she would want it for the newspaper. Yet it didn't feel right to let him leave without saying something to this man who had experienced love for half a century and wanted to tell everyone about it. It wasn't until Kim had laid out the paperwork on the desk and left the office, and Abby had turned back toward the window and watched Martin Rayfiel disappear across the town square, passing the gazebo without a glance, his linen suit lifting as if a simple spring breeze might carry him to another county, that Abby knew what she wished she'd called out to him.

"Happy anniversary," she said.

The next day Abby Reston went about the business of putting together another edition of the *Longwood Falls Ledger*. She oversaw a staff meeting, wrote an editorial on the debate over school taxes, edited copy, drank too much coffee, forgot to eat lunch, pulled herself from the depths of a late-afternoon blood-sugar low with the help of two Almond Joys, hated herself a little for eating two candy bars instead of the salad she'd stashed in the office minifridge that morning, and finally, at promptly 5 P.M., pressed the key on the computer that dispatched the May 28, 1999, edition of the paper off to the printer and into the world.

Which made today May 27. Abby got up from her desk and stretched her arms above her head, feeling something inside her lightly pop and crack. For the first time all day she thought about the enigmatic man who had paid her a visit the previous afternoon, and she thought about the one day a year that, for some reason, he and a woman named Claire were able to see each other. Abby glanced out the window at the white gazebo in the distance, as if Martin and Claire might have materialized there. But then she remembered: *dusk,* he'd said. It wasn't quite dusk yet, and even if it were, Abby didn't know what it was she hoped she might find outside her window except two people in love—not exactly an uncommon sight on the lawn of a town square.

So she got up and left the office, quickly walking the three blocks to her small clapboard house on Alder Lane. It was a luxury to be able to visit her daughter during the workday—something she'd never been able to do when she was a magazine editor in New York City. Now she let herself into her house, where Miranda, who was six, was sitting at the kitchen table, being served a plate of chicken nuggets in the shapes of various dinosaurs by the housekeeper, Mrs. Frayne.

"Mommy, look. Triceratops," Miranda announced, holding up a piece of chicken, and then she leaned across the table to embrace her mother. Abby inhaled the sweetness of her daughter: a chocolate milk smell, and a fruity children's shampoo.

Miranda talked of school, and Abby listened. Miranda's class had visited a dairy farm that day, and each child had personally given a tug at the udders of an oblivious cow, a fact that had Miranda chattering away. Abby sat down and leaned forward, her elbows on her knees, as if she was studying her daughter's face, memorizing it for the long evening ahead at the office. Miranda had her father's coloring, the Irish setter shade of brown hair and dark brown eyes. It was an odd punishment to be reminded of Sam whenever she looked at Miranda, but there it was, unavoidable.

Abby had never thought it would be easy to raise a child alone, but she hadn't realized how hard it would be to continually *leave* Miranda. There were always good-byes: another meeting Abby had to run, another deadline. It had been just as bad in New York City, and the only times she and her daughter had a chance to really be together were on weekends, or at night after Mrs. Frayne went home to the apartment she rented in a house two blocks away, when they would sprawl across Abby's big bed and talk for a long time. Abby would braid Miranda's hair and softly read to her. There was no pleasure as intense as this one, she would think to herself.

But now she had only a little while to catch a glimpse of Miranda and hear about her day, and then it was time to get back to the office. She touched her daughter's shoulder and got ready to leave. "See you, Mom,"

Miranda said, smiling, and then immediately dipped her head down to continue reading a book about a girl and her pet chameleon.

"Oh, Abby?" said Mrs. Frayne. "I almost forgot. Someone called before, from New York City, said his name was Nick, and that he just wanted to say hi and see how you and Miranda were doing."

"Nick the doctor?" said Miranda, looking up and appearing interested, and Abby nodded.

Nick Kelleher had left a few messages since she'd moved here, and they'd spoken twice, briefly, catching each other up on their lives, flirting in a light way, but she had never given him any real encouragement, never let him think that she was interested in him. Still, for some reason, he kept calling.

"He sounded nice," Mrs. Frayne said wistfully.

"He *is* nice," said Abby, and then she turned and headed for the door, abruptly ending the conversation. "See you later," she said to her housekeeper and her daughter before they had a chance to say anything more about Nick.

But on her way back to the newspaper,

the sky growing dim, the workday ending for most people though not for her, dusk really arriving, Abby paused on the green. It was true that she had to get back to work, but maybe this *was* work, she reminded herself: a story she'd been invited to write, the story of Martin Rayfiel and a woman named Claire. A love story, he'd said.

Abby selected a bench near the gazebo—not so close that she would seem intrusive, but close enough so that in a little while she would discreetly be able to observe the . . . what? Reunion? Rendezvous? The gazebo seemed an unlikely setting for something illicit: open and airy and more than a little old-fashioned. But maybe that was why they'd chosen it. Who would suspect that two people meeting in the most public place in town were trying to hide something? In fact, as she studied it now, Abby realized how little she'd ever thought about the gazebo. It was simply *there*. She had never before examined the delicacy of its architecture, the gingerbread wood painted white—an octagon, she noticed, counting—or the roof coming to a point that punctuated the sky beyond. It was an evocative if frivolous structure, yet apparently it had meaning to at least two people.

Abby leaned back against the bench and began her vigil. She saw a heavy, elderly woman in a cardigan and too much bright makeup, and she hoped this wasn't Claire. It wasn't; the woman kept walking. Good, Abby thought. Then another woman, red-haired and pretty and wearing a zippered jogging suit, approached and actually sat in the gazebo, but she looked too young to have been meeting Martin there for fifty years. In a moment the woman was joined by two other women friends, both of them in jogging suits, too, and the three of them stood, did a few leg stretches, and jogged off together. Then no one approached the gazebo.

The streetlights around the square popped on all at once, followed a moment later by the antique lamps along the lanes in the square. It was an appealing setting, and all of Longwood Falls, New York, was like that: idyllic in many ways, safe and intimate and scenic, full of greenery and ponds and winding roads lined by low fences. Yet in the end it had not been enough to hold her here. Like so many of her friends the summer after high school graduation, Abby Reston had boarded a southbound train to New York City with barely any regret.

Now she was back. When her father died of a sudden heart attack last fall, Abby had returned home for the funeral, and to help her mother. She'd brought Miranda and their housekeeper, and a few days evolved into a few weeks. Then she ended up staying on, moving back here, and taking over her father's job as editor of the *Ledger*, settling herself and her daughter and even their housekeeper, who hadn't loved the city anyway, into this very different life. Her coworkers said she worked excessively, and of course, they were right. Some of it was simply learning to readjust to the pace of a small town again. At the women's fashion magazine in Manhattan where she'd worked as a features editor, midnight closings were common, almost an excuse for a frenzied slumber party atmosphere of pizza and wine and complaints and exhaustion. Mrs. Frayne had often had to stay very late in the apartment back then, and Abby would give her cab fare and send her home in the dead of night. "You work too much," the house-

keeper had bluntly said as she shrugged
into her coat at 1 A.M., a comment that would
be echoed again and again by various people. But some of Abby's approach to work
was hereditary. It was a trait she had inherited from her father, and sometimes, sitting
behind the same heavy birch desk that Tom
Reston had occupied for forty years, Abby
couldn't help wondering if her father had
found solace where she did, in moments of
quiet efficiency and the formidable accumulation of facts.

This would have been his kind of story,
she knew. Abby felt certain that a tale of two
lovers reuniting every year for fifty years
was one her father would have run in the
newspaper. He knew what spoke to the
community. Whether it spoke to *him*—
whether he was capable of considering anything in any capacity other than as the editor
of the newspaper—was another question
entirely. Once, when Abby was a teenager,
she had asked her mother, "Who does Dad
love more, you or the *Ledger*?"

"That's a complicated question," her
mother had answered, after a long moment's consideration. "I think he loves us
both, but in different ways."

The answer stunned Abby. She had expected her mother to say something reassuring: "Why, *me,* of course, but your father sometimes has trouble expressing his emotions." But instead her mother had decided to give Abby a different truth, a more complete one, and in doing so she also had imparted an essential lesson: don't ask the question unless you want to know the answer.

The question Abby had come here to ask at dusk was primarily whether she wanted to run this story in the paper. But she'd also come to sit on a bench near the gazebo in the square now to find out what *her* response was—not as an editor, but as a reader. Did the story speak to *her*? Did it resonate? But time was passing, Claire and Martin hadn't shown up, and now, Abby supposed, she'd never know.

It was dark in the town square. The sun had slipped behind the stand of trees at the west end of the square, and then behind a cluster of storefronts. Martin had told her that he and Claire had never missed a meeting in the gazebo, not once in fifty years; Abby didn't know whether to be irritated or concerned. She considered calling the police, but what would she be reporting? She didn't know either of these people. Maybe one of them was busy and had told the other one this morning, and they had rescheduled their meeting for a different day. Maybe she'd missed them. By the time she returned to the town square from her house, they might have come and gone. Or maybe the whole thing was a hoax. But she couldn't quite believe that was the case. Martin Rayfiel, in the brief time he had spoken to her, had been earnest and forceful: an ardent, breakable man.

Abby stood and looked around. She was alone now. The shops that ringed the square on all four sides were closed, their shutters drawn, their gates shut. She walked over to the empty gazebo, climbed its two white steps, and sat down inside. She tried to picture Martin and Claire meeting there, embracing as they sat on the white wooden slats. Then she noticed something; it was underneath one of the seats, half hidden there. Abby bent forward, then got down on one knee to retrieve it: a briefcase.

She pulled it out of the shadows and set it on the floor of the gazebo. It was old and worn, but made of quality leather and stitching that had clearly lasted many years. She ran her fingers along the stamped letters of the monogram: *M.R.* This was Martin Rayfiel's briefcase, the one he had carried into her office the day before. Had he left it here for Abby to find? And if so, why? She looked around the square; she was still alone. She hesitated a moment longer, then reached for the clasps. The locks sprang easily, and she flipped the lid open.

The briefcase was filled with a jumble of items, many of them difficult to see in the dim light from the streetlamps in the square, and none of them meaningful to her in any way. It looked like the assortment of things you might find in a chest in someone's attic: old postcards, letters, restaurant menus, faded photographs, long-forgotten trinkets. She passed her hand over it lightly, fearful of disturbing some unseen order, until at last her fingers came to rest on a stack of several cassette tapes held together with a thick rubber band. She picked up the tapes, raised the stack to catch the light from a nearby lamp, angled it until she could make out the writing on the first tape. In an elegant script were the words, *Abby Reston— please listen to these first.*

It startled her to see her own name here. It was as if someone had suddenly whispered her name from out of the half darkness surrounding the gazebo, and for a moment she considered slamming the briefcase shut and shoving it back under the bench, as if she'd never been here, as if she'd never seen this. But she *had* seen it. She held the tapes in the palm of her hand, hefting them lightly, as if weighing her options. So she was right; he'd left the briefcase in the gazebo for her to find—or at least for whoever did find it to deliver to her. But did she really want to get involved? If she were to take these cassettes back to the office and pop them in the tape deck that sat on her desk, the one on which she often listened to Chet Baker or old Beatles songs or Chopin études, she would be in the thick of it—whatever *it* was. She wanted to know who Claire and Martin were, and why they hadn't come to the gazebo today. But how much did she want to know it? *Don't ask the question unless you want to know the answer.*

Abby picked up the briefcase as though it were hers and carried it back across the green. When she reached her office at the now-empty newspaper—her coworkers having all sensibly gone home to families and warm dinners and easy chairs and time away from their jobs—she tugged on the chain hanging from her gooseneck lamp, throwing a circle of light onto the chaotic surface of her desk. She cleared away the layout sheets and placed the briefcase down, then went to the refrigerator in the hallway and pulled out a bottle of Gewürztraminer wine that had been cooling there horizontally for several weeks, a present, she seemed to recall, from a satisfied advertiser—the owner of Shur-Foot Shoes for Big and Tall Men ("Widths to EEEE!"). She took a corkscrew from the drawer in the kitchenette, grabbed a mug from the dish drain, and brought it all back to her office. There, in the lamplight, Abby opened the bottle, poured a glass, and popped the first tape in her cassette deck.

"Hello," said the recorded voice of Martin Rayfiel. "If I'm right, you're probably listening to this tape in the evening, sometime after dusk, after you've realized that Claire and I aren't coming to the gazebo. I'm sorry to have disappointed you," Martin went on, "but the circumstances are very complicated, and can hardly be explained in any superficial way. So if you care to, I thought you might like to listen to the story that I have to tell about Claire and myself. I hope the items in the briefcase will help illustrate what I have to say, although some of them may strike you as absurdly sentimental, and you'll wonder why I've saved them all these years."

Abby reached under the desk to remove her shoes, letting them drop to the floor, and then put her feet up on the desk. The sound of the voice in the calm of an office after hours was oddly soothing, and as Abby took a first cold swallow of wine and leaned back in her chair, she felt it was a voice she could have listened to all night. And so she did.

CHAPTER TWO

Claire Swift never wore a hat. In winter when she was a girl, her mother would come chasing after her with a woollen cap in hand, frantically waving it in the air, but Claire would already be gone. Throughout her entire life, whenever Martin thought of her, he would always see her hatless head, hair swinging. When they first met, though, he did not see her at all.

It was Friday, May 27, 1949, Martin recalled on the tape, and he and Claire were both seventeen years old. They had grown up in the same small town of Longwood Falls, but their lives within the town were so different that they had never spoken. As Martin explained it, the division was simple: his family was rich; Claire's was not. She lived on a downtown cul-de-sac cluttered with small cottages and attended the local public school. He lived at the top of a hill in a neighborhood of enormous, ostentatious houses known as the Crest, and went to a formal boys' day school twenty miles away. Like these houses, Martin was constantly at a remove, suspended slightly above everything. But unlike the other people who lived in the Crest, Martin refused to isolate himself, and so he often ventured downtown, even though his wealth and his gray military-style school uniform made him an obvious target. On this particular occasion, Martin was buying himself a fountain Coke after school at Beckerman's, a local soda shop with gleaming taps, swivel stools, and an impressively varied jukebox, when he heard the first familiar comments: he was a queer. He should go back to the Crest. He should get on his throne and stay there.

They were local high school boys, and he had seen and fought them before, and soon he was fighting them again, throwing and receiving wild punches. Martin swung at one of them, his fist landing on a jaw with a terrible soft crunch, like biting into an apple. But the boy hauled back and punched Martin in the eye, and as the punch connected he felt a thud, a deep pain circulating inside his head, and then he was down on the white tiled floor, looking at the silver roots of swivel stools. Distantly, he heard the door stuttering shut, and the boys were gone. Beckerman himself, a worried middle-aged man who was always nervously wiping his hands on his white apron, helped Martin up and chiseled off a chunk of ice for him. Gratefully Martin took it and placed it over his eye, which had already retreated deeply into the flesh of his face, and then he wandered out into the day.

His family's driver, Henry, was waiting around the corner with the Bentley, most likely leaning against it and smoking, but Martin couldn't tolerate the idea of being ferried home, where his mother would make a foolish, woozy fuss over him, and his father would berate him for "engaging in violence with locals."

Instead, Martin Rayfiel walked into the town square, the grass giving slightly underfoot. Because it had rained the night before, the mineral smell of earth was now slightly stronger than usual. His eye was pounding with its own pulse and heat, and he somehow made his way to the gazebo. Martin had always liked the looks of the gazebo, the way it was poised in the center of the square, as if in the middle of nowhere. Now he climbed the white steps and lay down on the bench under the roof, his knees bent, his head resting on the smooth, varnished slats. Alone finally, he repositioned the piece of ice over his eye, and then he let out a groan. "Christ oh Christ," he said to himself. "Isn't this great?"

"I wouldn't say that," said a voice.

Martin sat up quickly. A girl was facing him, about his age, and her arms were crossed. She was smiling at him. No, she was smirking, and Martin braced for an insult, some sarcastic comment about his family, his money. But none came. Through his one open eye, he noticed the book on her lap, *Treasures of European Sculpture*. She was a good-looking girl in a peach-colored summer dress, her arms and legs long, her hair fair and straight, and Martin was embarrassed as only a seventeen-year-old boy with a swollen eye who has been talking to himself in front of a girl can be.

"You know," she went on, "I heard that meat works better than ice."

"Is that right?" he answered. She nodded. "Thanks for the tip," he said, and he stood carefully, trying to give himself some dignity, pretending that he was not in pain and that he could simply saunter out of the gazebo and back across the green.

"Would you like to try it?" she asked. "I live around the corner; I could get you a piece of steak."

He looked at her. "You don't even know me," he said.

"No, I don't."

"And you're inviting me to your house?"

She nodded to him.

"Why?"

"Because you're hurt," she said simply.

The girl was being kind, but she was also being playful, provocative. The mixture of these qualities made him curious, and to his surprise he soon found himself agreeing to be led to her house around the corner. The house was shockingly tiny, and surrounded by other houses just like it. Where did her family sleep? he wondered, looking around at the small, crowded quarters.

The kitchen was small but clean enough, and she produced a slab of raw steak for him, a cheap cut still in its butcher paper, and sat him down at the table, where he obediently placed it over his eye. He could smell the fresh meat as he held it across his face, the blood of it somehow disturbing him now. "I was in a fight," he explained to her, although she hadn't asked. "Actually, *they* were in a fight with *me*. I'm not even sure why it happened."

"I know why it happened," she said. "It's because of who you are."

"Oh? And who *am* I?" he said.

"I don't know your name," said the girl slowly. "But I've seen you around town. In that silver car of yours. And with your family. And I know that what happened to you today happened because of that. People get jealous."

He nodded. "That's right," he said.

"This has happened to you before, hasn't it?"

"Yes," said Martin.

"So why do you keep coming down

here?" she asked. "Going to the same places, letting everyone see you?"

He paused, thinking about it. "I guess," he finally answered, "it's also because of who I am." She looked slightly puzzled, but he didn't elaborate. He didn't know how to explain that the reason he came downtown again and again, the reason he often found himself in the center of pointless fistfights, was precisely because he refused to be isolated up on the Crest.

Martin had never felt comfortable living there, growing up in the vaguely ridiculous columned home that had been built to look like an antebellum plantation house. The veined marble floors were too slippery to walk on comfortably, and when Martin was small and pretended to ice skate across them, his nanny or one of the maids always made him stop. His parents employed an ever-changing domestic staff, whose leave-takings were largely related to the unpredictable moods of Martin's father, Ash Rayfiel, an imposing and demanding executive who had inherited the family business: ladies' hats.

As a result, Martin's mother, Lucinda, seemed to have more hats than any other woman in the world. The walk-in closet where her hats were stored had been expanded and was referred to as "the hat room." She owned high, fluffy hats that looked like meringues, and squat black velvet ones that seemed appropriate for a state funeral. She had an eggplant-colored hat studded with tiny seed pearl buttons, and a wide-brimmed yellow one that was the exact same shade as the buttercups that bloomed in clusters on the family's property, and it attracted about as many flying insects whenever she wore it. Lucinda Rayfiel was an abundantly unhappy woman, preoccupied with her hats and with her appearance in general, as a way of forgetting her unhappiness.

The main hub of the Rayfiels' social life was the Longwood Golf and Country Club, located on a rolling spread of gated property, and to which all the residents of the Crest belonged. Every Saturday morning, Henry carefully drove the family car down the hill and through town to Longwood Golf and Country, where Martin's father smacked ball after ball onto the greens, shouting vulgarities when he hit a sand trap, and his mother drank one stinger after another, letting the day slip by in a drunken fog, and Martin was left to his own devices.

He hated the club. The other children there seemed to him snobbish, unpleasant, or worst of all, dolts. They were miniature versions of their parents, he saw, and the idea that he, too, might become some version of his parents frightened him. His father was handsome but rough-edged, lacking subtlety. He was in a constant state of anger. Martin's mother, while elegant and blonde, had a droopiness to her features that kept her from being actually beautiful. She looked, Martin had come to think, like Rita Hayworth's slightly desperate older sister, if the actress had had one.

Martin resembled his parents only in some vague, oblique way. He was more introspective than either of them, and more distracted. His hair was straight and seal-black, and his eyes were gray with tiny lines and shapes embedded in the pupil, as though cut from a piece of his parents' marble floor tile. His body was equipped with a kind of litheness that enabled him to easily scale fences and run anywhere he had to faster than anyone else. It seemed to Martin that he was always running, always escaping from someplace or other.

It occurred to him, as he sat here at the kitchen table with this girl, that he didn't want to escape from her house. To his surprise, he just wanted to sit here at this small, shaky table all afternoon. His eye was starting to feel better, and he removed the steak and set it back on its damp square of paper.

Suddenly the kitchen door opened, and a man walked in. This was the girl's father, handsome but weary, his T-shirt soaked through under the arms with half-moons of sweat. He smelled strongly, too, although it wasn't only a smell of perspiration. There was the mineral smell again that Martin had noticed walking across the green: dirt, and lime, and something else with a sharper note to it. Paint, he realized, and turpentine.

The man looked at Martin with an unreadable expression, then slowly nodded hello. "Claire," her father said, "would you get me a beer, please? And maybe you could start my supper. Your mother says she splurged and bought me a little steak."

So her name was Claire. The name seemed right, a simple, easy fit. She and Martin exchanged guilty glances. The steak that had been pressed against his wound would now be cooked and eaten—a vaguely disgusting but funny thought that they shared. "I'm Martin Rayfiel," he said to Claire's father.

"Ash Rayfiel's son?" he asked, and Martin nodded. "I've done some work for him," Claire's father continued noncommittally, although Martin knew what he was thinking. It was what everyone thought of Ash Rayfiel: he was a bad person, no friend to the working men and women of the town. There had been rumblings, intimations of reprisals against Martin's father, but because he was so powerful, nothing had ever come of these comments.

Martin was embarrassed, and tried to change the subject now. "Your daughter," he explained, "helped me out today."

"She's a helpful girl, I guess," was the reply. Then Claire's father took the amber beer bottle by its neck and carried it out of the kitchen. Within minutes, Martin imagined, he would be fast asleep somewhere with his feet up.

"I should go," said Martin.

"Yes," said Claire. "I guess you should." But he didn't move. They smiled at each other, because neither of them wanted him to go, and they both knew it. He was unnerved by this girl with the fair hair who just sat there across the table, watching him, amused. She was playing, and he was excited by the odd little game.

The way he felt reminded him of something that had happened to him two years earlier. There had been a cook in his parents' house named Nicole Clément. She was a woman from a small town in the south of France called Lourmarin. She couldn't be described as beautiful, exactly; her hips were a little too full, and her dark hair always unruly, but she was attentive and welcoming. He often stayed near her in the kitchen while she stirred a copper pot of sauce or julienned carrots with a hand faster than a casino dealer's. She taught Martin everything she knew about cooking, and when his parents were away he hovered over her in the kitchen, in the middle of the fragrance and the noise and the steam piping up from pots if you lifted a lid an inch. Nicole Clément showed him how to pound the air bubbles out of bread dough, and how to cook a perfect egg. Martin became an excellent cook, with a deft hand at preparing both

French and American dishes. While his mother was somewhat amused at his skill, his father merely thought it was a girlish parlor trick and not something that could help him in the world.

One day, when Martin was fifteen years old and Nicole was twenty-six, he had stood beside her at the table, helping her slice potatoes. Suddenly he turned to her, saw the pastry flour that dotted her hair like fresh snow, and the way her hands moved quickly, rounds of potato flying. Before he even understood what he was doing, he leaned forward and kissed the cook hard on the mouth. Her eyes opened wide, but within a moment Nicole had set down her paring knife and was frantically kissing him back. Soon she moved into the pantry with Martin. Together, on the floor of that small room, surrounded by cans of stewed tomatoes and jars of jam and hanging ropes of garlic, Martin and the cook undressed each other quickly, in absolute silence.

When they emerged from the pantry sometime later—he had no idea how much time had passed—Martin stood tucking in his creased white shirt, sweeping back the lock of hair that always fell into his face, and taking a long breath. It was as though he understood that he would never become a hat man like his father, and that he would never live a life of country clubs and finance and deep unhappiness. He turned and saw Nicole standing nearby, quickly trying to re-tie her apron. He went over to her, because she looked frightened at what had just happened.

"You don't have to worry," he told her.

"Thank you, Martin," she said, pronouncing his name in the French way, as she always did. "You are very sweet, you know. A real 'catch.' "

Within a month she was gone. Nicole left her job, insisting that it had nothing to do with Martin, only that she missed her family in Lourmarin. He wasn't sure whether or not to believe her, but she cried when she left and said she would write to him, which she occasionally did. The new cook was a stout, bossy woman from the Swiss Alps who sang marching songs and grated cheese into every dish she made. While Martin picked up occasional cooking pointers from her, they never became friends.

After the experience in the pantry, he was quieter, more directed. Some sensation had come over him that day, and now, in another kitchen on the other side of town, it had returned. He suddenly wished he could lie down in a small, fragrant room with this girl named Claire. He could imagine his life being shaped around her; he wanted that to happen, though he had no idea why.

It occurred to him that people didn't need to be exactly like each other in order for a strong current of feeling to pass between them. His parents liked to socialize only with people who were just like them; he had once heard his mother discussing, in a low, meaningful tone to a friend of hers at the club, another woman who was supposedly "not one of us." Which meant, it turned out, that the woman wasn't wealthy and was therefore ineligible to join Longwood Golf and Country.

Martin wanted to be with this girl Claire, who was clearly "not one of us." He liked that she was different, that the things she knew were clearly different from the things he knew. And yet he felt that they were oddly similar. It was time for him to go now, and yet he still couldn't bring himself to leave. For some reason he was stalling, lingering, loitering here in her house. Instead of saying good-bye, what he said to her was, "Can I cook the steak for your father?"

Claire stared at him. "You know how to cook?" she said, her voice full of doubt. He nodded. "You do not," she said.

"Yes I do."

"You're kidding, right?" she asked, and he shook his head no. "Okay, be my guest," she said, shrugging and gesturing that the kitchen was his.

He took over in the narrow space, slicing cloves of garlic and cubes of butter on a cutting board the size of his hand. When he asked Claire if there were any spices handy, she said there were some herbs growing in a patch beside the house. She picked some for him, then brought them back inside. He minced onion grass and wild thyme and made an herb butter for the steak, which he rinsed well, since it had been on his black eye. When the steak was done, Claire regarded it with surprise, for not only was it clearly delicious, it was also artfully arranged on the plate. She brought it silently in to her father, who happily ate it up, announcing later that it was the best dish she had ever cooked for him.

Afterward, when the kitchen was still fragrant, and the day was almost over, Claire turned to Martin and told him he had to leave. "This time I mean it," she said. "My mother will be home soon from the fabric store with my older sister, Margaret. And unlike my father, they'll ask a million questions."

"I wish they would," he said softly. "I'd tell them anything. My shoe size: eleven. My intelligence: fairly high. My—"

"*Go,*" she said firmly, and she opened the kitchen door for him.

"Claire," he said suddenly. "Meet me at the gazebo tomorrow."

Suddenly she wasn't smiling anymore. "No," she said. "There's no point. We're totally different."

"So what?" he said. "Please. Just meet me."

She looked at her hands, lacing them together, deciding. "Not tomorrow," she said. "Next week. Same time."

"Fine. Next week," said Martin. They stood in silence at the half-open, curtained kitchen door. He didn't want to ruin this afternoon. It was like a recipe, he thought; if you stirred too long, you would change the consistency. So without saying another word, he walked out the door of her kitchen and didn't look back. Next week, he thought to himself as he walked down the path to the little cul-de-sac, whose name, he saw from a sign, was Badger Street. Without realizing it, his step became quicker, until he was practically running. Next week, he thought. *Next week*.

The Rayfiels' driver, Henry, was waiting by the car several blocks away, smoking and looking very concerned. He dashed the cigarette out under his foot. "Are you all right?" he asked as Martin climbed in beside him. It was not the first black eye he had seen on this boy.

"Yes," said Martin, and he leaned his head back against the brown leather seat of the Bentley, one eye as big as a plum and swollen shut, as the car began its ascent up the hill toward home.

During the week, Martin was entirely distracted, performing poorly on an English examination and making a crucial error in chemistry class that almost resulted in a sulfurous explosion. The headmaster, Mr. Croft, invited Martin into his office for "a word." Croft was a decent man who was close to retirement, and Martin did not want to disappoint him. "I know you're headed to Princeton in the fall," said Croft, appraising him from beneath a wall of diplomas, "but still it's essential that you keep your grades up to the level at which they have been all along."

Since meeting Claire, Martin had entirely stopped thinking about the fact that he was going away to college in September. He had been accepted to the school his father and grandfather had attended. From the time of Martin's birth, it was assumed that he would eventually go to Princeton, where he would join the same selective eating club that the Rayfiel men had always belonged to, and that he would do everything that they had done: play varsity football, study economics, and date a certain type of extremely rich, dull girl with strong teeth and a throaty, slightly hysterical laugh.

"I'm sorry, Mr. Croft," Martin said to the headmaster. "You're right; I've been distracted. I'll try to be more attentive." But he was upset now at the idea of going off to college in the fall and leaving behind this girl Claire, who he hadn't yet gotten to know.

When next Friday came around, Martin

did not have Henry drive him into town. Instead, after school he changed out of his uniform and into a casual shirt and pants, then headed down from the Crest alone, on foot, telling no one where he was going. He walked lightly across the green, afraid that she wouldn't be there, that she would have forgotten. Or, worse yet, that she hadn't forgotten but had just changed her mind and decided not to come. He almost couldn't bear to look, but now, as he approached, he did.

In the distance stood the gazebo, a simple, octagonal white structure that seemed half made of air. And inside it, she waited for him.

CHAPTER THREE

The rich boy with the black eye came into Claire Swift's life in a way that took her by surprise. It hadn't occurred to her that she might fall in love while still living in her parents' home. She had imagined it happening in some distant future, far away from this cramped house and the absolute lack of privacy that was the defining feature of her girlhood. Claire supposed she had known she was in love with Martin from the moment she invited him to her house for a steak to put over his eye. But she kept this knowledge hidden from herself at first, convinced she had only been trying to be "helpful," the way her parents had raised her to be, and that she would have behaved exactly the same way regardless of who had stepped into that gazebo with a black eye.

Still, when she was about to see him a second time, she was nervous to the point of feeling frantically sick to her stomach. *Butterflies,* the sensation was called, but the word seemed much too frivolous to describe what she felt. They sat for a while in the gazebo, and then they walked half a mile to a meadow, where they sat again. He wanted to know all about her, and she told him about her family, and how, when she was eight years old, she'd almost died of spinal meningitis, and how she wanted to be a sculptor—taking an advanced art class at school, and always winning first prize in the annual student art contest. He in turn told her about his family, and about wanting to be a chef, and about how he was reluctantly going off to Princeton to study economics in September, when what he really wanted was to go to cooking school. They exchanged a round of details and asked each other questions in a big hurry, as if to make up for lost time.

They agreed to meet again the following

afternoon, this time at a nearby pond where they could go swimming, even though it wasn't quite swimming weather yet. When she arrived the next day at the side of the pond at three-thirty, he was already there, sitting on a rock with his shirt off. She briefly took in his long arms and bare chest with its feathering line of dark hair. Soon they were in the cold water together, touching the slick bottom of the pond with their toes, their skin rippled with gooseflesh, knees lightly bumping.

Finally, after they had stood wading and shivering in the pond for a good five minutes, he came closer, as though crossing the line of the invisible circle that all people inscribed around themselves. But somehow, she didn't want him to move away.

"Hello," he said to her.

"Hello," she said in return.

He was going to kiss her now, she knew, and to her surprise the sickened feeling returned. She wasn't sure why she felt this apprehension, but it was a part of who she was. Claire's mother had always been overprotective, chasing after Claire with woollen hats and offering warnings about men.

"Don't trust them," her mother had said. "You're a pretty girl, and they will try and sweet-talk you into things you may regret."

She heard her mother's words now, although they were the last thing she wanted to think about. Why should she trust Martin? There was really no reason. Claire knew that his father, Ash Rayfiel, had a reputation around town as a ruthless businessman—in fact he had cheated her own father once, something to do with payment for a garden wall. But this moment, here in the still, cold water, had nothing to do with reason. Martin put a wet hand on her shoulder and brought her even closer to him. Claire immediately felt the heat and color of her face climbing until it reached her hairline.

Of course she wanted to kiss him, too, but she was only seventeen years old and was alarmed by this urgent feeling. Boys at school had always shamelessly flirted with her and asked her out and called pleadingly to her from across the athletic field as they ran around tossing balls, and she had gone to the Longwood Cinema with several of them, including Roy Crenshaw, who kissed her in the balcony during the newsreels. Roy was a lazily handsome basketball player at

Longwood Falls High with wavy blond hair and sleepy eyes, but she had felt very little during his kiss, only a bit of anxiety about whether other people in the theater were looking, and a slightly unpleasant awareness of the taste of butter on his lips and tongue, for Roy had been eating handfuls of popcorn.

But when Martin kissed her, standing in the pond, she felt everything. Martin's mouth touched hers, then he backed away slightly and approached again from a slightly different angle, off by a few degrees. Roy Crenshaw had smelled of some awful pine-scented hair tonic that he had glugged freely onto his hair from the bottle, but Martin wore no scent. He smelled like a handsome boy in sunlight: something sweet from the tail end of childhood mixed with something darker and more adult. Sweet and sour, she thought giddily as they kissed. So this was what it was all about, she realized, all those desperately romantic movies she had watched with her sister at the Longwood Cinema, all those things that characters in movies always claimed they felt for each other. She thought of her own luck in discovering him, in discovering this feeling.

It woke up something inside her that had been asleep her entire life. It shook it awake, as if saying: *It's time*.

Martin and Claire quickly developed a routine that allowed them to see each other at least three times a week, sometimes four. Any less than that gave Claire a panicky sense of need and withdrawal. Even when she did see him, she was slightly unhinged. I have become a deranged person, she thought to herself one afternoon during sewing class at school as she wildly scattered a zigzag stitch across the pocket of an apron she was making, ruining it. Then high school ended for both of them, and summer began. Claire slept late every day. Sometimes she slept until one in the afternoon, lying in bed and thinking about Martin until her worried mother came to the door and asked if she was okay.

"I'm fine," said Claire, but still her mother came in and placed the back of her hand against Claire's forehead.

"Well, your head is cool," said her mother, eyeing her curiously.

Once, when no one was home, Claire took Martin to her house to show him one of her small clay sculptures that her parents kept on the mantel. It was of a girl sitting by herself and reading. Martin admired it, knowing right away that the girl was Claire as a child, created from memory. She wanted more than anything to be a sculptor, but her parents couldn't afford to send her away to art school. She was very talented, and they knew it, but even if they could have sent her, she told him, they probably wouldn't have. The Swifts were conventional people, and they naturally assumed that their daughters would get jobs in Longwood Falls after high school: perhaps doing some of the lighter maintenance work for their father, or even becoming a receptionist in a local doctor's or dentist's office. That was what Claire's older sister, Margaret, had done since graduation, answering telephones and managing the front desk for the elderly, forgetful Dr. Somers. Margaret didn't particularly like sitting all day at the desk behind the sliding frosted glass window, listening to the phlegmy coughs of patients in the waiting room, occasionally getting up to replace the array of magazines with newer ones, or to feed the sluggish goldfish that swam in a tank by the window, but she never complained. Still, the idea of a similar future was very depressing to Claire, especially now that she had met Martin.

"Let me ask you something," Martin suddenly said to her one afternoon in the meadow. "If you had money, and no restrictions at all, and didn't have to worry about what people thought of you, what would you do with your life?"

"Oh," said Claire right away, "I would definitely travel. Go to Europe and take a tour of all the great art there, and study sculpture for real." She paused. "But it's so ridiculous to think about this," she said. "I don't even have a passport. I've hardly ever been out of Longwood Falls."

"Europe," said Martin, who had been there several times with his parents, "is absolutely nothing like Longwood Falls."

"What would *you* do?" she asked him.

"I'd go with you," he said without hesitation. They were both silent. During all the afternoons they'd been meeting, they hadn't really discussed the inevitable, but it lay ahead of them whether they liked it or not. In September Martin would be going to Princeton, and Claire would be staying behind, finding a local job and living at home, her life remaining static, with nothing much to look forward to. But Martin's life would keep moving forward, taken up by studying and term papers and spirited football games and wealthy girls. On weekends he would dance with these slender girls who had strings of cultured pearls encircling their slender, white throats. Claire didn't know which was worse—the idea of sharing him with *them,* or sharing him with anyone.

They didn't talk much about their upcoming separation in the fall, politely ignoring it as though it would go away on its own. He had no desire to go to Princeton, wishing instead he could go somewhere to learn to be a chef and take Claire with him. She, too, wished she didn't have to listen to her parents. Her mother in particular was always watchful and frightened, as though convinced that something bad would inevitably happen to her younger daughter.

Claire's father was less worried. He was preoccupied by his work, which was constant and difficult. Lucas Swift was a maintenance worker employed by the town to garden, prune, and plant as well as to repair sidewalks and fences and maintain the gazebo in the middle of the square. He had recently enlisted a cousin to help him with his work, and now the two men were calling their business Swift Maintenance, which they had stenciled across the side of a truck. The work was increasingly demanding, and Claire's father came home at the end of the day in a sweat and feeling like a dog who just wanted to curl up and sleep. The Swifts were a struggling family but not impoverished. Once in a while there was an inexpensive steak in the refrigerator, and though the household wasn't fueled by laughter and play, at least everyone got along. They were not one of Tolstoy's happy families, but they managed.

Happiness, in fact, had always seemed like a somewhat false concept to Claire. She'd been a slightly melancholy girl all her life, yet when she was alone with Martin she knew happiness wasn't false, only elusive. But now she had caught it by its wriggling tail, and here it was in the form of this boy with dark hair and a fading bruise and expressive hands. They continued to tell each other things, including the most personal stories from their lives; he even told her about his afternoon spent on the floor of the pantry with Nicole the cook.

Claire and Martin didn't talk about their feelings for each other to any of their friends, and Claire never mentioned it to her older sister, Margaret, but it was inevitable that people would find out in such a small town as Longwood Falls. They had been seen together often enough, and one day the talking simply began, an energetic cicada whirr of it among both the people in the Swifts' social class as well as up on the Crest.

"What's this about your daughter and that millionaire boy?" the checkout woman at Stover's market bluntly asked Claire's mother, Maureen Swift, one afternoon as she stood on line. "It's nothing but trouble, if you ask me, not that you have," the woman went on. "The father's a bully, and the mother drinks, and everyone knows they're the worst snobs in the entire county."

Claire's mother, who didn't know anything about it, pretended that she did. "Oh, it's all just talk," Maureen said smoothly as she picked up her grocery sacks and collected her change, but that evening in the kitchen, standing side by side with her daughter as they washed a hill of supper dishes together, she confronted Claire, who first bit her lip, denied the accusation hotly, then immediately broke down and told her mother the whole story. A lifetime of dutifully telling the truth to a demanding mother could not be reversed in one evening.

"I love him, all right?" she said, the words tumbling out.

"Well then, learn to *unlove* him, Claire," her mother said. "There would be too many problems; it would be awkward. Everyone would be so unhappy about it, and you'd only end up terribly hurt."

Claire angrily dried a plate with the thin checkered rag in her hand. "Love doesn't work like that," she said to her mother.

"I'm well aware of how love works," said Maureen quietly. "Young people always think they're the first ones to discover love, but believe me, it's been around before you and it will be around long after you're gone from the earth." She paused. "But when it takes place between two people who have no business being together, then it will always make their lives miserable."

"It's not love that's doing that," Claire said. "It's *you*." And with that she flung down the dishrag and stormed off to her bedroom.

Meanwhile, up on the Crest that same evening, Martin was told in no uncertain terms that he was never to see "that girl" again, whom his parents had learned about through a vulgar and wealthy widow at Longwood Golf and Country named Velma Cornby—a woman, Martin had always thought, who because she had no life of her own feverishly gossiped about everyone else's.

"Let me spell it out for you, nice and clear. Your mother and I forbid you to continue seeing that girl," said Ash Rayfiel after calling Martin into his study.

Martin faced his father across the big desk with its oxblood blotter, surrounded by books Ash Rayfiel had never made the time to read. Books that, by their sheer number, were designed to impress visitors, and that was all. "You *forbid* me to see her?" Martin said, and Ash Rayfiel nodded. "Sorry," said Martin, "but I thought we were past the 'forbidding' period of my life. I thought I got to make my own choices by now."

His father stared at him, unblinking, then poured himself a drink from a cut-glass decanter shaped like a pear. "All right, Martin," he said. "Then sit down for a moment, and we'll talk." He poured his son a big glass of bourbon and handed it to him. Martin had never had a drink with his father before. They sat on the stiff leather couch, and Ash finally said to him, "If you insist on seeing her despite our protests, I suppose I should be relieved, in a way."

"How so?" Martin asked.

"Because it shows me you're normal," said Ash. "Your mother and I were a bit worried about your development, what with that cooking you like to do." He took a long drink of bourbon. "If you keep on seeing this girl, I guess it's because she has something very . . . sweet about her, if you follow what I'm saying. And the sweetness of the honey is what counts, isn't it?" Ash nodded to himself. "It all tastes the same, rich or poor, and what's the harm so long as you don't knock her up, although I'm sure we could do something about that too—"

Martin put down his own glass of bourbon and stood. "You don't know anything about Claire," he said. "Or about anything."

"Oh, I know loads more than you think," Ash said in a quiet voice. "But you can't see that right now. Someday, maybe you will. But here's the truth: if you let her, which you seem bent on doing, that girl is going to ruin your entire life."

"Thanks for the advice," said Martin. And he turned and left this cold room with its walls of unread books.

"So I guess you're planning on letting her!" Ash Rayfiel called to him, but Martin didn't answer. "Fine! Go right ahead!" he heard his father shouting as he descended the stairs.

Claire and Martin became more discreet over the course of the summer, meeting less frequently and in places where they felt fairly certain they would not be discovered. They no longer met out in the open in the gazebo during the day, or even in the meadow, or by the pond. Instead, they met miles away in the far woods on the periphery of Long-wood Falls, a place visited by the occasional trembling deer and by very few people. The woods were thick here, and there were mosquitoes dotting the air. They usually planted themselves in a tangle of branches and leaves. It was darker in the woods than in the places they were used to, for the sun couldn't find too many openings to poke into between all the trees. The woods were like a dark, slightly forbidding bedroom. Sometimes Martin posed for Claire here when she asked, taking off his shirt and letting her sculpt him from a few scoops of red clay that she had brought with her in a tin.

Claire was miserable in the woods, and she said so. She was upset that she and Martin had to go so far away to be alone together, that they couldn't walk hand in hand through town like other swooning couples in love. And it was all because of money. She didn't want Martin Rayfiel's wealth or status, though some people in town had suggested she did. She wasn't looking to marry "above her station," to leave behind the life of being the daughter of a man who pruned hedges and repaired sidewalks and painted the gazebo for a living, upgrading to be a rich man's smug, idle wife. It was said in town by some of the smaller-minded citizens that Claire Swift was trying to buy her way out of what she'd been born into. Only when she and Martin were alone together did the rumors and passing comments fade into a distant, insignificant chatter.

And then summer was almost over; now a new kind of urgency infused their time together. One day at the end of August, as they lay in the woods, Martin turned to her, propping his head on an elbow, and stopped talking. "What is it?" she said.

"You know what I'd like? To be with you for an entire day," he said. "Someplace that's not here. Someplace where we can lie together without goddamn stupid pinecones sticking to our clothes."

"Where?" she said.

"The Lookout."

Claire sat up and stared at him. "We can't go there," she said. The Lookout was one of those two-story motels off Route 9 with peeling aqua paint and an old pool that had remained empty for years, filled with trash and cobwebs.

"It will be okay," he said. "It's probably nicer on the inside. I just want to be with you," he went on. "We don't need to do anything you don't want to."

She turned away from him. The truth was that she wanted to be with him in a place that wasn't covered in a thicket of branches, too. She wanted to sleep with him. But this went against everything she had been taught, everything that was appropriate for a girl of seventeen to feel in 1949. Her parents—her mother especially—would have been horrified by her desires. Her mother would have wept and begged her to change her mind, and would have chased her all the way to that sleazy motel with a woollen hat in her hand.

But now Claire stopped thinking about her mother. In an uncertain voice, not looking at him, she said to Martin, "It's okay; I'm not offended. I want to be with you, too, you know."

"Then you understand what I'm saying," he said, and after a moment she nodded. "You constantly amaze me," said Martin.

The following Saturday, they hitchhiked to the motel, and a milk truck picked them up on the side of the road. They sat stiffly in the back among crates of fresh milk, hearing the bottles rattle and chime lightly all around them. Claire wore a dress her mother had made that was the color of cocoa—a pale brown, powdery shade.

They were posing as a married couple. "Newlyweds," Martin had told her giddily, slipping one of Claire's own inexpensive silver bands on her ring finger. "We're the Harrisons of Saratoga Springs," he'd improvised. "John and Alice. We were married in Saratoga at the Adelphi Hotel. A fairly small wedding, two hundred people or so."

"So what are we doing at the horrible Lookout Motel, if anyone asks us?" asked Claire.

"Oh, we're just exploring upstate New York," explained Martin. "Wandering around like any two people in love, enjoying being aimless before we get down to the seriousness of our life. We're staying in little motels—the kinds of places that are missing letters in their neon signs."

The Lookout was missing its first *o*. Claire shook her head and said, "All right, John. We'll go to the Lookout."

"Thank you, Alice," he said. "You won't regret it."

They each had brought a small suitcase for authenticity; surely the Harrisons would have clothing with them. Claire kept her overnight case primly on her lap during the bouncing milk truck ride. Inside there was only a cotton nightgown with a row of rosettes lining the border, although she knew she wouldn't be wearing it. The driver of the truck let them out right at the gravel entrance of the motel. There were a few cars parked in the lot, and the place didn't look particularly sinister, but still Claire felt afraid. At the front desk they signed their aliases in the guest register, and the old woman in a hair net on duty didn't even cock an eyebrow in suspicion. She didn't care who came through here, as long as they weren't violent and didn't destroy the furniture, and as long as they paid for their room.

"Oh, one more thing," Martin said to the woman at the desk. "Is there a room with a kitchenette?"

She looked suprised; probably nobody ever asked for such a thing. "It'll cost you seventy-five cents extra," she said, and he agreed to pay it. The woman slid a room key across the counter, and that was that. In silence, Martin and Claire walked back outside and climbed the rickety wooden staircase to room 18.

The door was an ugly aqua color, with shredding curlicues of paint. All Claire could think about was that her father could have repainted that door nicely, the way he took care of the gazebo and some of the fences around town. Inside, the room was dim and musty, as though no one had been there for weeks. The bed in the middle of the room sagged, but it seemed clean enough.

Claire wondered how she had gotten herself to this point, and she considered turning around and leaving, not saying a word. Everything here was so unfamiliar. But then Martin came close to her; there was that sweet and sour smell again, and the assured clasp of his arms around her, and she remembered that *he* was familiar. She had already memorized the feel of him, his voice, the things that preoccupied him. He was not a stranger, and so she told herself she didn't need to feel that everything around her was strange.

She undressed silently in the dim of the motel room, and he watched her, what he could see of her. "You're just beautiful," he said, and then he took off his own clothes and slowly pulled back the blue coverlet of the bed, and they both slipped inside. It was cold in there, like the pond. The room was hushed and shadowed even in the middle of the day. She felt that they were just two swimmers in the water. He kissed the hollow of her clavicle, then moved lower until his mouth was suddenly on her breast. She breathed in sharply and felt herself grow tense, every muscle in her body alert and tight, but then she reminded herself: *I am Mrs. John Harrison, a married woman.* His mouth stayed on her breast. Claire heard herself groan; was that really her?

Their clothes were gone, had drifted off somewhere into the darkness, and now it was just a collision of warm skin against warm skin, pale surfaces against darker ones. Then there was inevitable pain, a shiver of it, bright and frank, which made her turn her head away for a moment, but then it, too, was gone, and what remained was a sensation like floating in clear water. Martin gazed down at her, his dark hair falling in his face.

"I love you, you know," he said.

"I love you, too," she said.

"We'll always belong to each other," he said. She knew that there was an implicit second half to his sentence, that he was saying: We'll always belong to each other *even when we're apart*.

Later, when they were lying together quietly, Martin got up from the bed, still undressed, and went to his little overnight bag. "What are you doing?" she asked, because she had imagined that they both might nap awhile. But he was taking some objects out of his bag and then carrying them over to the hot plate in the kitchenette, for which he had paid seventy-five cents extra. An onion, a couple of eggs he had swaddled in a handkerchief in his bag so they wouldn't crack, a stick of butter, a wedge of hard farm cheese, a mouli grater, a pair of silver salt and pepper shakers with an *R* engraved on the side of each one, and, finally, a small skillet.

Claire watched in surprise as this naked man stood and cooked an omelette after lovemaking, his hands quickly slicing and working. When it was done, he slid it onto a plate and came back to bed. They sat eating and leaning against each other, wishing they could find a way to be suspended in this moment forever, here under the thin blue blanket, in a room in a seedy motel with the missing *o* in its neon sign.

Martin was driven down to Princeton on a wet Sunday morning. The trunk of the car was packed full of Martin's suitcases and his steamer trunk, and Martin sat in the backseat beside his mother, who wore a leafy green hat that reminded him of a cabbage head, and who, as the Bentley pulled out of the Rayfiels' driveway, immediately poured herself some liquor that was stored in the car's compact bar. His father had declined to accompany his son to his first day of college, insisting that he had previous obligations relating to his hat business, but Martin knew it had to do with the angry conversation they'd had in Ash's office that summer.

During the ride, Martin looked dully out the window while his mother smoked and complained about the declining quality of membership at Longwood Golf and Country. The long car pulled through the wrought-iron gates of Princeton in the early afternoon as the college carillon bells were clanging in the distance and young men and their parents explored the campus.

In the solid stone building where he was to live, Martin met his roommate, a bony-faced boy with bad skin who was from Durham, North Carolina, and named Everett P. Hudson Jr. The two of them unpacked their things, and Martin's mother fussed around the room a little, trying to be helpful, and then she was off, saying something about a dinner dance that night at the club. She kissed her son's cheek, barely touching it with her lips, and he realized that her love had always been like that: well intentioned but vague, and slightly missing its mark.

Later, when Everett had gone down to the entering students' sherry hour, having unsuccessfully tried to persuade his roommate to join him, Martin sat alone in his new room on the striped mattress ticking, looking at the elaborate moldings and staring over the campus with its Gothic spires and its ambient sense of self-importance and infinite possibilities. Somewhere on this campus at this very moment, Albert Einstein was sitting and thinking up earth-shattering equations, or else perhaps just taking a shower. Martin reached into his jacket pocket to fish out his keys and loose change, and as he did, his hand brushed against a piece of paper. Surprised, he withdrew it from his pocket and looked at it.

It was an envelope with nothing written on the outside, but when Martin brought it closer to his face, a scent drifted up: *Claire.* The soap she used, something citric smelling, like both lemons and oranges. He quickly tore it open, and began to read:

Martin,
Where are you right now? Are you in the car with your mother? Or are you sitting in your room? Either way, I can't believe

you're not here with me. Will we ever get
to Europe? I love you.

Claire

He sat and stared at the brief letter, picturing her sitting in her cramped bedroom at
home and writing it. Over the next weeks
and months she would write many more letters to him, most of them longer, more de-
tailed, and he would immediately write back.
Martin tried hard to throw himself into his
studies; classes were lively, and he was taking European History, Introduction to Poetry,
Plant Biology, and Latin. But the letters from
Claire were much more compelling than any
of his schoolwork. All around him swarmed
young male voices: in the high-ceilinged
classrooms, at his eating club, where plat-
ters of food were passed by silent black
waiters, and after hours, when the young
men gathered in dormitory rooms to play
poker and smoke cigars in their underwear,
knock back expensive scotch, and talk dirty
about women. Martin joined in the card
games and was well liked, but he was considered opaque, which suited him fine.

He came home for Christmas and then
again for spring break, and although he had

a great deal of studying to do during vaca-
tion, he spent most of his time with Claire.
He knew his grades would suffer, but he
didn't particularly care. She had taken a job
working as a receptionist for a local dentist
named Dr. Mantell, who was nice enough to
her, but the work was dreary. Patients came
in with toothaches and left with their mouths
numbed and thick-tongued from anesthetic;
it was no life for Claire, but it would have to
do for now.

During Martin's vacations, the two of them
went back to the Lookout Motel a few times.
Sometimes they sat in the gazebo, or skated
on the now-frozen pond. Claire was exactly
as she had been when he had left. Princeton
had a great deal to offer, but it couldn't provide Martin with the two things he knew he
wanted: to be with Claire, and to become a
chef. Still, he resigned himself to passing
each year of college with the thought that he
could be with Claire all summer. In this man-
ner, Martin managed to get through three
years at Princeton.

On the day before final examinations in
his junior year, Martin and his roommate for
the past three years, Everett P. Hudson Jr.,
were getting dressed, when Everett sud-

denly turned and said in his thoughtful drawl, "You've never really been here, have you?"

Martin regarded him. "What do you mean?" he asked.

"You're somewhere else, I think," said Everett, knotting his tie with the tiny orange Princeton tigers on it. "Somewhere better."

Martin nodded. Today was May 27, 1952, three years to the day that he and Claire had met at the gazebo. They ought to be together today, he knew, as they had managed to be every year on the anniversary of their first encounter. They ought to be together today and every day. They ought to travel to Europe, to see it all. For three long years he'd slogged through school, resenting the separation, and now he knew it was time to change things. He didn't want another year to go by during which they would be apart.

In two hours he was supposed to begin a round of examinations, writing his long answers in the blue books that all students were given. There was no point to this, for he would not become a scholar in his life, or advance to law school or business school. "I'll see you later," he said to his roommate, and then he walked out of his room and onto the campus.

The place was oddly quiet; everyone was inside studying. Martin walked and walked down to the playing fields, where a long time ago his young father had once kicked a football, and where, an even longer time ago, his grandfather had done the same thing. Martin sat down on the grass, and that was when he saw the man. He was walking along with his hands behind his back—a rumpled old man in a navy cardigan with wildly sprouting white hair and a mustache. He appeared to be lost in thought. *Albert Einstein,* Martin realized.

He imagined going up to this brilliant, world-famous physicist and pouring out his heart to him. Perhaps Einstein would have something consoling to say, something philosophical and transcendent that would put Martin's problems in perspective. But Professor Einstein was walking away, his hands shoved in his pockets, already lost in some spiral of thought that Martin couldn't even begin to imagine.

Martin gazed after him. Then he suddenly stood and broke into a run, heading away from Einstein, away from the college entirely, across the expansive green playing fields and directly over to the Western Union Office in town, where, his hand shaking slightly, he stood and wrote out the following telegram to Claire Swift:

COMING HOME TO YOU FOR GOOD STOP MEET ME AT GAZEBO AT EIGHT STOP MAR- TIN

That evening, May 27, 1952, a soft, wind- less night in upstate New York, Martin stepped off a train onto the platform at the Longwood Falls station and walked across the town square to the gazebo, where Claire sat in a sleeveless dress the color of butter. He buried his face against her shoulder. "For *good*?" she asked quietly, and all he could do was nod.

CHAPTER FOUR

Abby pushed the pause button on the cassette player, stopping Martin Rayfiel and his story in the middle of a sentence. She had been sitting at her desk, legs up, not moving, for the better part of an hour now, and as she shifted in her chair she felt lightheaded—whether from the wine or the lulling effects of Martin's voice, she couldn't say.

Abby sat straight in her chair and pulled herself closer to the desk for a better look at the photos that lay at the top of the stack of things inside Martin Rayfiel's open briefcase. First she saw an old, faded black and white photograph of a shyly pretty girl; on the back Abby read, written in a careful hand, "Claire 7/12/49." Next she found a picture of a handsome boy, someone right on the precipice of adulthood. It was Martin, she knew, and he was as striking when he was young as she'd imagined. In the picture he was standing against the sloping silver side of a car, his arms crossed, tall, lean, black haired, and transparently, soulfully unhappy. And no wonder: when Abby turned the photograph over, she saw the words, "Martin on his first day at Princeton, 1949."

Abby looked further, found a few other photos: Martin in front of his parents' house, Claire with her sister, Margaret, in their little yard, but none, in this top layer of things in the briefcase, of Claire and Martin together. Of course not, Abby thought; they had no one who approved of their relationship, no one they could speak to about it, no close friend to whom they could casually hand a camera and say, "Would you please take our picture?"

Abby kept searching through the top layer of objects and papers. She found the letter that Claire had written to him his first day at college. The handwriting was just as she'd imagined it: careful, curved, identifiably feminine. Abby lifted the piece of paper to her nose, and she could have sworn that, after all this time, she still smelled the very last traces of the citrus soap that had scented everything Claire touched. She set the paper aside, with the photos, and next lifted out of the briefcase several ancient pink carbon-copy slips: receipts for motel rooms at the Lookout, signed in 1949, 1950, 1951, and 1952 by a Mr. and Mrs. John and Alice Harrison of Saratoga Springs, New York. The motel was gone now. Abby remembered when it had been razed some years ago and replaced by condominiums. Then Abby found the telegram from Martin to Claire, dated May 27, 1952, its edges frayed, the paper as delicate as an old doily.

And there, right beneath the telegram, she found two faded gray tickets—halves of tickets, really. Stubs. The printing on the stubs was very faint, and Abby had to squint to make out some of the words. *Idlewild* she saw, and *Orly,* and *May 28, 1952.* So they'd gotten to Europe after all. And only then did Abby realize how much she'd been hoping they had. They'd boarded an airplane and gone to Europe, eager, thrilled, terrified.

Abby remembered this same mix of sensations, this feeling of starting something entirely new. It had happened to her once, and she hadn't had to travel to another continent to experience it. Nine years earlier at a jammed art opening in New York City, she had seen a tall man leaning against a wall, perilously close to an ugly painting of a screaming monkey. He held a plastic cup of the type of bad wine you find at art openings, and he was talking easily to a cluster of people. She noticed him—his deep brown hair and eyes, the way he was making the others laugh—and then he noticed her noticing him, and soon he was slipping through the crowd to Abby's side of the room. For a few seconds they stood in silence, pretending to look at the paintings.

"So," he finally said, "do you like screaming monkeys?"

He was an art dealer in from Los Angeles, she was an editorial assistant on the rise, and Abby had thought, quite reasonably, *This is it*. And Sam Bachman *was* it, for a while anyway. They had never had to struggle with the idea of "love." It had come early, and easily, and often. They said it giddily to each other several times a day on the

phone, and then they said it in person almost every evening they were in the same
city together, and even when they couldn't
say it, they said it anyway. "I love you" said
the note in the candy bowl, "I love you"
said the note in the soap dish, "I love
you" said the note in her change purse, and
when Abby looked back on their two years
together and strained to figure out what had
gone wrong—why she'd believed everything
she'd believed—she wondered what else
she could have done, in the face of so much
evidence.

But that's just what it was in the end: so
much evidence, a paper trail that would
have been persuasive if all she needed to
appeal to was reason. For one mad moment, sitting on the couch with Sam in the
living room of her one-bedroom apartment
on the fourteenth floor of an anonymous
building on the West Side of an anxious city,
she actually had thought of producing the
notes—of disappearing into the next room
and grabbing the seemingly bottomless
shoe box full of all the testaments to his love
for her that she'd saved and overturning it in
a snowfall of folded white paper as if to say,
See? See? See? As if the sheer volume of

the evidence was all it would take to change his mind, to make him want to stay with Abby and raise the baby she was going to have in eight months.

Instead, she sat in silence and let him have his say. "If you choose to do this, then that's it between us," he said. "I'm sorry, but I won't have any more to do with you." Sam was like a different person, sitting rigidly and unmoving on her couch. Gone, in one breathtaking instant, was the easy grace of the tall man leaning against a gallery wall, making everyone laugh; in his place sat a stiff man, cold and unbending. "I'm not ready to be a father. If you think you're ready to be a mother, fine. That's your choice. But," he added, "I won't have anything to do with the child."

The child. Sam had elevated the potential baby right out of adorable babyhood and into the slightly less innocent waters known as childhood, and in that moment, the fight went out of Abby. *See? See? See?* she could say as much as she wanted, and now she knew his answer wasn't going to budge: *No.* Sam stood, said "Think it over," and turned and left her apartment. Abby sat for a few more minutes, unable to stand, or call a friend on the phone, or cry, or do much of anything. She was newly, accidentally pregnant, but she already felt changes deep inside her. *Think it over,* Sam had said, and she did. She would have this baby, this child who would eventually turn out to be Miranda Rose Reston. But Sam, somehow, was lost to her forever, a fact that, in many ways, Abby still couldn't quite comprehend more than six years later. She had loved him, had allowed herself to be consumed by him, and then he was gone, just like that.

Abby stared now at the photo of the young, sad Martin, missing Claire on his first day at college, and she thought of the man who had appeared in her office the previous day. They were the same man, of course; yet how was that possible? She thought of her own father, too: back then, a slightly remote young man in a soft flannel shirt; now, gone for good. Then Abby picked up the photo of Claire from that faraway summer, and she looked into the eyes of a girl who had long ago grown into a woman, and then eventually into a woman who, like Martin Rayfiel standing in her office doorway the previous day, must now be nearly old.

But still in love. And that was the difference between the love story that had been unfolding before her all evening and any- thing Abby might ever encounter in her own life: she knew how it was going to end. She could stare into the faces of the man and the woman in the photographs, side by side on her desk, and know what she couldn't know gazing into the eyes of a man at an art opening in New York City: Fifty years from now, you're still going to be in love.

"Mrs. Frayne?" Abby said on the phone, a moment later. "Listen, something's come up here at the office."

"Don't tell me," the housekeeper an- swered. "I should make up the guest room and get myself comfortable."

"Would you mind?"

"All night?"

Abby regarded the stack of audiotapes on her desk, the pile of photos still in the brief- case. "Could be," she said, her voice apol- ogetic.

When she hung up, Abby began the tape again, and as Martin's voice resumed the story, she played with the photographs of Martin and Claire on her desk, moving them closer together, until they touched.

*   *   *

Martin and Claire weren't eloping exactly.
They were doing something far more daring,
for Longwood Falls in 1952 anyway: they
were traveling to Europe together, a man
and a woman, unmarried—no longer Mr.
and Mrs. Harrison, but not yet Mr. and Mrs.
Rayfiel, either.

The plan, when it was hatched, was simple and apparently faultless. The next day,
Martin would collect an object from his family's safe—something that belonged to him
and which he could easily sell in Europe and
live well off for several months. Claire would
bring her birth certificate and the passport
forms Martin had gotten for her to the bank,
in order to get the forms notarized there, so
she could get a passport in New York City,
then fly to Europe at night. The money he
already had in his bank account would cover
their airfare. When Martin turned twenty-one
in the fall, he would collect his entire inheritance, and he and Claire would be able to
live off that money for as long as they
wanted. In Europe, Martin could learn to be
a chef, tasting everything, peering into the
kitchens of restaurants in city after city, and
Claire could study sculpting. Their life, as

they imagined it, would have no clearly defined limits.

"There's one thing," she said to him as they sat at the gazebo and made their plans. "What about getting married? We haven't really talked about it very much."

Martin looked at her, clearly startled. In a soft voice he said that he knew they would be married eventually, but he saw no hurry for it right now. He liked the idea of not getting married immediately, of living a life that seemed, by the standards of the day, unconventional. "We'll get married when we've decided to settle down somewhere," he said to her. "How does that sound?"

She said it sounded fine, but she was very apprehensive. It was as though fragments of her mother's personality were making an appearance in Claire. She was willing to go off with him to Europe—something she had dreamed of—but still she was afraid. She didn't know how she could say good-bye to her parents and her sister. Would she sit them all down in the tiny living room and announce her news? No, it was much better just to *go,* she realized, leaving behind a note on the kitchen table that explained what she had done, and telling them not to worry about her, though of course they would. She wasn't a little girl, she was twenty years old; so why did she feel so guilty?

Now Claire and Martin parted until tomorrow, the day they would head down to New York City by train to fly out of Idlewild Airport in the evening. After they separated, Martin went home to his family up on the Crest, and his parents were shocked to see him. So as not to make a scene, he lied and told them that he had taken all his examinations the day before.

His mother, through the veil of her drinking, seemed to believe him, and his father only raised his eyebrows and said nothing. But late that night, when Martin was sitting in his room, he heard a heavy tread on the carpeted stair. He looked up; his father was leaning against the door frame of his son's boyhood room and peering inside, looking around at the old framed prints of jungle animals on the walls and the swimming and baseball trophies on the shelf, all of which seemed to Martin to be relics from someone else's childhood, not his own. "So," Ash Rayfiel said, "how were your final examinations?"

"Not too bad," said Martin stiffly.

"Glad to hear it," said his father. "I re-member how difficult they could be. Sitting there for hours, hunched over a desk, sur-rounded by other men, everyone incredibly nervous, and all you can hear in the big room is the squeak of pens on paper."

"Right," said Martin, looking at the floor.

"Look at me, Martin," said his father, and Martin's eyes moved upward, to where his father stood.

"You're a pathological liar," said Ash Ray-fiel calmly. "But I guess this girl of yours doesn't mind. It goes well with her own char-acter flaws. What does she care that you dropped out of college the day before final examinations, that you lied to suit your own little needs? All she cares about, I guess, is the money. My hat—so to speak—goes off to her."

"You're wrong," said Martin.

"Am I?" said his father. "Look, you have to face it. This is a girl with no advantages. Zero. A girl who imagines that she was des-tined for a better life, except for the incon-venient fact that she happens to be the daughter of a maintenance man. So she gets it into her head that *you* can be the one to change everything, that *you* can make her life a whole lot better. And she desperately pursues you. And because you're inexperienced and gullible and apparently dying to get under her skirt, you take the bait."

Martin sat very still and straight in his chair. Finally, when his father was done speaking, he asked, "How did you get to be so suspicious of everyone? Were you born that way, or is there something in the water of this town?"

His father looked amused. "Hard to say," he replied, and then he paused, changing the subject. "The dean at Princeton called me," he said. "That's how I found out about what you did. Your mother, however, doesn't yet know. She was at the club when the call came, so she's not yet aware of your stunt."

"When are you going to tell her?" asked Martin.

"I haven't decided," said Ash. "Soon enough. She'll be heartsick, of course."

"Well," said Martin, "I guess she can heal her sickness with vodka." He immediately regretted the casually cruel remark.

Ash gazed steadily at his son. "You have a choice," he went on. "You can continue down this self-destructive path, or else you can return to Princeton in the morning. You've been granted permission to take all your examinations tomorrow afternoon in the dean's office without penalty, so long as you show up on the dot of three o'clock, appropriately remorseful."

"What did you do to get the dean to agree to that?" asked Martin. "Did you offer to donate hats to the entire faculty for the rest of your life?"

"Never mind," said Ash quickly. "It saved this family from embarrassment. And that's all that matters." Then he turned and descended the stairs.

Martin walked over to his bed, knowing that this would be the last night he would ever sleep here. As he lay down, staring up at the ceiling, his toes touching the carved footboard, the thought of leaving this too-big house and this too-small bed made him immensely, surprisingly, sad. He had never liked it here, and now he was leaving; the sentimental feeling seemed to come from nowhere, but still it kept him up half the night.

Down the hill, over on Badger Street, he envisioned Claire living out the last hours of

her own girlhood, furtively packing the clothing and birth certificate she'd taken from the
bedroom she had slept in since she was
born. On her bed were a few stuffed animals
that had belonged to her as a little girl. All
of them had been stitched and restitched
over the years, and regardless of what color
they had once been, they were all now the
color of the gray slush that covered the
ground when the snow began to melt in
Longwood Falls each spring. Claire would
be leaving behind this room that she used
to share with her sister: the vanity table with
its clutter of bottles of toilet water and hair-
brushes threaded with fine, fair hairs, and
various tubes of lipstick, the ends long ago
blunted. Lucas and Maureen Swift would be
disturbed and mournful over the loss of their
younger daughter. But it wasn't as though
Claire would be dead. She would be more
alive than she had ever been before. In fact,
she'd be different.

At nine in the morning, after his father had
left for work and before his mother was
awake, Martin met Claire at the row of
hedges in front of his house up on the Crest.
He had asked her to come here at this hour

without telling her why, and although she was frightened, she'd agreed.

"I have to tell you something," she began before he could even speak. She was studying her hands. Red clay had lodged under several of her fingernails. "I couldn't get my birth certificate. I was positive it would be with my parents' papers in the closet in the front hall, but it wasn't there, and I couldn't exactly ask them where it was, or they'd know something was up, and I—" She stopped, unsure of how she could possibly cushion the disaster.

Martin held her shoulders, then hugged her. "All right," he said, and he realized she was crying. He could feel the rise and fall of her shoulders against his chest. "It's all right. We'll think of something."

"I like how you said that," she said. "The *we* part."

Still, though they were a "we" now, getting to Europe wasn't going to be as easy as they'd thought. Martin and Claire entered his house through the service entrance, where the fat Swiss cook was grating a hunk of cheese the size of a dictionary. As they went past, the cook looked them over with narrowed eyes but just kept on grating, her arm rubbing hard at the huge piece of cheese, shavings flying fast into a bowl. Martin led Claire out of the servants' area and down a marble hallway that shone like a dark lake, and into the cherrywood dining room.

"What are we doing here?" she whispered, but he only put his finger to his lips. On the wall in this room with its long, formal, highly polished table in the center hung a Frederic Remington painting of some long-dead man on a long-dead horse. Martin lifted the painting carefully from its hook. "God, you're stealing it?" Claire whispered, shocked, but he shook his head no and smiled, revealing the wall safe hidden behind the painting. Martin dialed the combination swiftly, then he turned the handle of the gunmetal gray safe, and the door opened. Inside the darkness of the small vault were various securities and bonds and bound stacks of paper money. Finally his fingers encircled what he was looking for: the gold Rayfiel family heraldic crest, which was practically breaded in diamonds and lapis lazuli. It was a gaudy, ugly piece, about six inches by nine inches, that had been commissioned by Martin's great-grandfather

Simon Rayfiel a long time ago, and it was meant to be mounted on a wall or lent to a museum. It had belonged to Martin since he was born, though he'd never once given it a single thought.

But now he took the object, holding it in the palm of his hand. If his father was going to throw the weight of his money around, then Martin would do so in return. It would be a silent game of catch between father and son, a dialogue without words.

Claire was staring at the object. "I've never seen anything like this in my life," she whispered.

"Yes, isn't it incredibly ugly?" he said, and he slipped the crest into his jacket pocket, closed the safe, and returned the painting to the wall. Then, just as he and Claire were leaving the room, he heard a sound in the hallway.

Turning, he saw his mother. She was wearing a long brocade robe, belted loosely, and her blond hair was uncombed, her eyes groggy. She looked both fragile and ruined; drinking had changed her, so much so that Martin barely had any memories of her that didn't include the stem of a glass being clutched in her careless hand.

"Martin?" his mother said.

Suddenly a memory broke through to him, just a fragment, really, from his early childhood: his mother embracing him before she and his father went out to the club for the evening. He remembered the gleam of her pearls and could feel her hand resting warmly on top of his head. He had thought she was the most beautiful woman in the world.

"What are you doing, dear?" she asked now.

"This is my friend Claire," he said softly, not really answering her question. "And we've got some things to take care of."

"Oh, I see," his mother said, but she didn't see, of course, and her voice sounded hungover, lost. She stared at Claire for a moment. "She's lovely, Martin," she said in a whisper, as though Claire wasn't there at all.

"Yes, isn't she?" he answered, and then they were gone.

There was one difficult task to take care of: getting Claire's passport application notarized without a birth certificate. Together they walked into Hudson Valley Trust and Loan, and Martin asked to see the manager, a Mr. Clendon. He explained the situation, showing Clendon the documents, explaining that Claire's birth certificate was missing. But after peering at them for a long time through his rimless glasses, the manager shook his head. Coughing lightly, he said that in the absence of her birth certificate, the papers could not be notarized.

Martin looked at the bank manager, and he begged him to make an exception just this once. "Look, I know her well," he said. Then he went on, "Come on, you know my family, you know me. Can't you notarize the papers without a birth certificate just this once?"

But the man shook his head. "That would be illegal," he said, and he pursed his lips. "Now perhaps I ought to give your father a call and sort this out with him."

Martin thanked him anyway and quickly ushered Claire out of the bank. For lack of anywhere else to go, they went to the meadow, lying stunned on the grass, barely moving. "I want you to know that I'm very, very sorry," he finally said to her. "I told you that we could go to Europe. You were will-ing, and I've disappointed you. I didn't do my research; I didn't know there would be this problem."

"It's okay, Martin, really," she said. "It's my fault, too. I was wrong about where my parents keep my birth certificate."

"It's not your fault."

"We tried," said Claire, "and it didn't work." Then she added, "Maybe this is a sign. A sign that we're not supposed to go."

"A sign?" he repeated. "There are no such things as signs." He came closer to her. "Don't back out now," he whispered. "Please." She didn't reply. "Look," he said, "let me try one more thing. Will you wait here for me?"

After a moment she nodded. "Where are you going?" she asked.

"To see a friend" was all he said.

When Martin returned a while later, he brought with him a tall young man about his age with restless fingers and a nervous expression on his face. "Claire," said Martin. "This is the person I was telling you about. I've always called him Hush, because he's the quietest person I've ever known."

The man smiled and shook Claire's hand. She liked him at once, felt his seriousness of purpose. "Look," Hush said, "Martin told me you have a little passport problem, and I said I'd try to help." Hush had recently passed the notary public examination. He was the youngest notary public in this entire region, Martin told Claire, and if it was ever found out that he had notarized an application in the absence of a birth certificate, he would lose his license and be in significant legal trouble. But he took a breath and then stamped, sealed, and signed the pages of Claire's application in all the right places.

"You're on your way," he said when he was done, handing over her papers.

"I can't tell you how much we appreciate this," said Martin. "Now Claire and I can get the hell out of here once and for all."

Claire regarded Martin's friend for a long moment. "I'm curious," she said to him. "What made you decide to do this for us? I know it's illegal. I know it's a big risk."

Hush shrugged. At first he didn't say anything, but then finally he looked down at his hands and began to speak. "I met a girl myself this summer," he said softly, "and we're getting married in the fall. Everybody I know thinks the whole thing is great. Her parents love me; my parents love her. And *I* love her, obviously; she's got a great laugh, and she can whistle through her teeth, and she's a beauty." He paused a moment, looking up, then added, "If I couldn't be with her, I don't know what I'd do."

Claire and Martin tried to thank him again, to tell him that they would send him gifts from Europe, and was there anything in particular he wanted—maybe some glassware, or a scarf for his fiancée—but Hush held up a hand. "Please," he said, embarrassed. "Just go. You have a plane to catch."

Near midnight that night, Claire and Martin were on a transatlantic flight. They sat in their high-backed first-class seats, stiff with unacknowledged terror and almost not daring to speak or touch the trays of food in front of them. Claire had never flown before, so her terror also had something to do with the fact that she was improbably suspended thousands of feet above the water. For Martin, though, the terror was pure; he had wanted something, and now he had gotten it. And what he had wanted was taking him away from his life as he knew it. In his Introduction to Poetry class at college, he had learned that the great poets often considered love to be "transporting." Right now, he thought, love was transporting him and Claire across an entire rolling ocean, away from the singsong cadences and rounded edges of childhood, and all that was familiar, that was known.

When the airplane touched down in France at Orly Airport in the brightness of day, Martin turned and kissed Claire hard on the mouth. "This is it," he said.

"This is it," she repeated, though neither of them really knew what "it" meant. A while later, they had checked into their room at the George V. The bellman had shown them where everything was—even, to their amusement, the pull for the drapes, and the hot and cold water faucets on the sink—and then they had tipped him well, and he had retreated, murmuring. Outside were the muted bleats of French car horns and the occasional whistle and rapid burst of shouting, and the rows of trees and the ubiquitous presence of the Eiffel Tower, looking down over everything, Claire thought, like a watchful mother.

Her own watchful mother was far away, out of reach, and here in this hotel room with the cream-colored walls, the scroll-shaped pillows, the bidet in the bathroom, and the gauze curtains blowing in the open window, it was just the two of them: an exhausted man and an exhausted woman collapsed on a soft bed with their feet up, waiting to see what would happen next.

CHAPTER FIVE

At night, the monuments of Paris were illuminated by individual white beams, each one glowing until midnight, when the lights were unceremoniously snapped off, the show over until the next night. Claire wondered if Parisians felt the same sense of wonder as she did when they looked up at the milkily lit Obélisque, and Notre Dame, or whether they simply took it all for granted, as she had long ago started to take for granted the lesser, unilluminated sights of Longwood Falls.

She and Martin stayed out each night at least until the lights were extinguished.

"Good night, Notre Dame," Martin said as they stood on a bridge, watching the cathedral fall into darkness. "Sleep well."

Sleep was not something they themselves actively pursued. Paris in 1952 was a good place to be young and American and wide awake. The city had recovered from the war, mostly returning to what it had once been, and anyone with a certain degree of kinetic energy, romanticism, and pocket money came here now. They flooded in from the States, and in every café or *boîte* you could suddenly hear a plainly American accent rising up over the clashing of glassware or the insistent syllables of people speaking hurried French.

At first, Martin and Claire shied away from other Americans, wanting to be alone together in this new city, to forget that they had ever lived anywhere else. They had the money that Martin had gotten for his family's crest from an old, distinguished dealer who had sat on a stool and peered for a long time through an eyepiece at the gems studding it. It was actually a great deal of money, allowing them to live in style into the late fall, when Martin would turn twenty-one and be able to claim his full inheritance.

One afternoon, he took her to the Chanel boutique. The large rooms were cool and fragrant, and though Claire was at first reluctant, he ushered her inside and could see the interest in her eyes as she looked all around her at the clean lines of fabric, the towering European models who wandered like gazelles grazing on a plain, the other women who were casually browsing. The men stayed on the sidelines, and Martin went to join them, his arms folded. It was like a strange, provocative sexual ritual, he realized: the women entering the dressing rooms and slipping into finery, then stepping out from behind the pale curtains to show the men their new, heightened selves. The women preened; the men appraised. Someone brought around a tray of drinks for the men, and Martin took a glass, as though he were at a cocktail party and not standing in a store. Claire was trying on a suit the color of green apples. It occurred to him that he compared most colors to food—no, he compared most *things* to food; he couldn't help himself. The suit was perfect on her, though she refused the matching hat that the saleswoman brought forward.

"Non, non," Claire said, holding up a

hand. She still hated the sensation of a hat on her head, though she insisted it had nothing to do with the fact that his unpleasant father sold hats. She just wanted nothing to hold her sheaf of hair down; she wanted to feel free all the time.

And she did feel free here in Europe; she told him this after they left the Chanel boutique with a glossy shopping bag packed with tissue paper and an apple-green suit that was so expensive it frightened her. They were walking along the Seine, Claire swinging the bag, Martin feeding the birds small pieces of a brioche he had stuck in his pocket at the end of their room service breakfast this morning. She looked so happy, he thought as he watched her. He had never seen her look like this back in Longwood Falls. Even that first day at the gazebo, there had been something guarded about her, held back, invisibly fastened down. Now she was opening; he wondered what she would open into.

That night, Claire wore her Chanel suit, and Martin wore a new slate linen jacket, and they had dinner in a tiny restaurant in the Champs-de-Mars district called Solange. The room, which looked out over a garden, was lit by small scented candles, and the waiters moved silently across the beams of the floor. The food, Martin said as they ate, was perfect. It wasn't revolutionary cooking; no shocking duos of flavors were brought together for the first time on the plate. The meal was simply excellent: everything about it, from the bread hidden in its envelope of folded napkin in a basket to the sole dotted with capers, to the salad that gleamed with good oil and wine vinegar, to the smelly but appealing cheese plate, to the delicate pear tart that sadly ended the dinner.

Martin didn't talk much during the meal but just studied the experience, looking around him, watching the way a waiter stood poised with bread tongs, watching the way another waiter confidently boned a fish in one sweeping gesture, watching the way a third opened a bottle of wine and stood patiently by while an elderly man took a slow, deliberate first sip. This was how it was done, he thought to himself, and he knew that he wanted to have his own restaurant someday. It wouldn't be in Paris, though, for he could never become proficient enough at French cooking to dare to understand all its complexities. But wherever it was, he thought it would resemble this tiny jewel of a restaurant.

Claire watched him watch the room. "You're working, aren't you?" she asked, and he nodded.

But her words had brought him out of these thoughts. Now he was with her again, looking across the table with its candle in the center at the pretty American girl in Chanel. He brought her hand up to his mouth and kissed it. "Thank you for putting up with me," he said.

"There's nothing to put up with."

"I know I get lost in myself sometimes," he said.

"So do I," said Claire.

Earlier that day, as they were walking to their hotel after shopping, he had seen this happen. They were passing a movie theater where, of all things, *An American in Paris* was playing. The movie had won the Academy Award the year before, and now here it was in a plush Paris theater. "Want to?" he asked, and she shrugged, and they went inside. They had seen the movie back at the Longwood Cinema the year before, sharing a big box of Milk Duds and enjoying it immensely.

But this afternoon in Paris the movie made Claire cry. In the darkness, Martin turned to her in surprise. "Are you okay?" he whispered.

She nodded that she was, but a while later he saw that she was still crying a little, and when he asked her if she wanted to leave, she said yes, she did. Out in the sunlight again, she couldn't really explain her reaction. The movie, after all, was a musical, with lots of dancing and singing and optimism. "I'm not homesick, exactly," she said as they walked back to the George V. "There's nothing in particular I miss. I was truly ready to leave home. I couldn't stand it there anymore." She paused, thinking hard. "But it's the only place I really, really know. And I feel that maybe it will always be the case."

He didn't try to argue, to tell her that soon she would know all the *arrondissements* of Paris as well as she knew the neighborhoods and roads and ponds of Longwood Falls. She was an American in Paris, and while that was certainly a lucky thing to be, it had its moments of sudden sadness and dislocation, too.

One day, Claire and Martin were befriended by another young American couple who had seen the *Treasures of European Sculpture* under Claire's arm, and figured that she spoke English. "Excuse me," said a slender blond-haired man on the steps of the Notre Dame cathedral at the end of a morning of sight-seeing. "Are you by any chance Americans?"

"Is it that obvious?" asked Claire.

"Oh no," said the pretty woman who was accompanying the man. "In fact, I said to Wally that you were both much too stylish to be Americans. I figured you to be European, maybe Scandinavian or something. But then we saw your book, and heard you speak to each other."

"You found us out," said Martin.

Soon the two couples—one from Longwood Falls, the other from New York City— were having lunch at a café nearby. Although Claire and Martin had been studiously avoiding other Americans, Claire seemed cheered by their presence. Wally and Kate were unmarried, too; they had lived in Greenwich Village in a fifth-floor walk-up apartment, where he spent the day working on his play, and she wrote strange pieces of modern music for the harp. Both of them had held night jobs in New York to pay the rent and save for their trip to Paris; she had been a telephone operator, and he'd bused tables at a coffee shop. They were here in Paris until their money ran out, part of a loose-knit group of other would-be writers and composers and artists who were living here in cheap *pensiones* or apartments. When Wally asked Claire and Martin where they were staying, Martin was vague in his answer, suddenly embarrassed by the truth.

Late at night Claire and Martin went with them to a party at one of these apartments on the Left Bank. The halls and the stairwell were filled with chattering Americans; the place was smoky as a nightclub and stank of whiskey. A fat, drunken young man from Kansas took a tumble down the staircase and had to be helped to his feet. Claire heard a man and woman passionately arguing about art; the fight, as much as Claire could tell, seemed to be over who was the better draftsman: Picasso or Braque. Claire had only recently been introduced to the work of these painters, and she was embarrassed. She wanted to be an artist, and yet she was way behind in her education. So far, walking through the wide halls of the Louvre with Martin, she had been over-whelmed by all she was seeing. But there was so much more; she would never see it all, she had started too late.

It was *always* too late, she thought. At the point when you actually realized something important, the moment to do anything about it had already slipped by. She had found Martin when she was seventeen years old. That shouldn't have been too late, and yet she knew that in some ways it was. Her fam-ily and her past already had a lifelong hold on her. She had cried at *An American in Paris* because the movie reminded her of what she had given up. She was different from Martin. He could make the break more easily; his family was awful, and their values were awful, too. She watched him now across the stairwell at the crowded party. He was talking in an animated way to two other men—something about the difference be-tween American and European politics—and he was smoking a Gauloise that one of the men had offered him from a flat blue tin.

Martin hated cigarettes. Yet here he was, easily taking in the experience of being young and impatient and standing on someone's packed stairwell on the Left Bank of Paris with a lit cigarette in hand, absorbing it all into himself. He had nothing to lose. He had broken with his family, and he was on his own; he would become very wealthy soon enough. But Claire was more afraid than he was, more homesick. She felt as though she still had plenty to lose. That was the difference between them.

A would-be novelist in a black turtleneck approached Claire on the stairs now. She had heard him discussing his manuscript with someone else earlier. It was called *The Taste of Bitter Pomegranate*, she remembered. "Enjoying yourself?" he asked her, passing her a tray of cheese that was so runny it was practically drinkable.

"Oh, yes," she said over the music, which was strummed chords of folk guitar along with some plaintive, mournful French lyrics that she couldn't understand. There was an awkward pause. "So," said Claire. "Your novel . . . *The Taste of Bitter Pomegranate*. That *is* the title, right?" He nodded. "What does it refer to?" she asked politely. "The pomegranate. Does someone in the novel actually eat one, is that it?"

The man stared at her for a long moment.

"No," he finally said. "There is no pomegranate in the novel. It's just a metaphor. Obviously." And then he turned away to find someone more interesting to talk to. Claire felt her face grow hot; she was both embarrassed and confused.

That night in bed in the hotel, Claire and Martin rustled and turned under the sheets, but neither of them could sleep. He had had a good time at the party; she had not. Both of them smelled of smoke. "Let's go somewhere tomorrow," Claire said suddenly.

She could see Martin clearly in the moonlight that came in through the tall windows. "Sure," he said. "Why not?" He was like that: easy to be with. Claire was slightly sad and restless, and Martin was willing to make a change whenever necessary. So in the morning, after consulting a map and a guidebook and the concierge, they were on the train to Aix-en-Provence. City slowly changed into country, and when they got off the train, they rented a bright yellow Citroën and drove over a series of small hills to the town of Lourmarin, where, Martin casually said, he knew someone.

"Who?" Claire asked in the car. "Who do you know?"

"Just an old friend," he said at first.

They stopped for a snack in one of the outdoor cafés along the way. Martin had a tall lemonade, and Claire ordered a frozen dessert called a *mystère*, which the waiter dug up from a freezer full of various kinds of ice cream. The *mystère* consisted of an orange with the pulp scooped out and replaced with orange-flavored sherbert. As Claire ate, her long spoon suddenly clacked against something hard buried inside the sherbert. "There's something in here," she said.

"Oui, mademoiselle," said the waiter, who had overheard. "It is a prize."

So this was the mystery of the *mystère*. Claire sucked at the spoonful of sherbert until her prize could be seen. "Oh, look," she said softly to Martin. In her hand she held a ring. It was cheap, made of tin with a green glass "jewel" in the center, and it caught a fragment of the afternoon light. They gazed at the ring, and Claire knew they were both thinking about when they would be married.

They had agreed that they would get married when they had decided to settle somewhere. They would marry and have a houseful of children. But when would they find somewhere to settle? In many ways, Claire was more conventional than he was; she needed to know that they would be settled soon, she needed assurance. "Of course it's going to happen," he had said to her repeatedly.

"When?" she'd always asked.

"Soon," he'd answered. Now he took the ring from her hand and solemnly slipped it on her finger. The ring was still very cold from having been inside a freezer for days, perhaps weeks. Martin leaned across the round metal table and whispered the answer to the question that she wasn't even asking at the moment. *"Soon,"* he said.

The old friend in Lourmarin, Martin finally admitted to Claire, was Nicole Clément, who had been the Rayfiels' cook and, for one afternoon, Martin's lover. Her name was now Nicole Vachon; she had married a local auto mechanic named Thierry Vachon. This much Martin had learned from Nicole's occasional, chatty letters. But he did not know much more about her, and it had been five years since they had seen each other. Claire, to his relief, was not upset.

"It will be interesting to meet her," was all she said.

When they arrived in Lourmarin, he'd hoped it was the kind of village where, if you stopped three or four people on the street, one of them would know the whereabouts of the person you wanted, or at least the family. And it was. The first person, in fact, a man wearing a long white apron and sweeping the street in front of a *boulangerie,* said yes, yes, pointed toward a steeple, and told Martin to turn left there and then ask anyone. Which Martin did, except for the asking part, because when they turned up the street past the church, there she was.

"That's her," said Martin. "I think."

The woman was walking away from them, up the hill toward the end of the street. A child was tugging on either hand, pulling her back, singing a song. *"Lundi matin,"* both children sang in high, clear voices, *"l'empereur, sa femme, et le petit prince . . ."*

Martin turned off the ignition, and he and Claire stepped from the car. He looked at Claire. She nodded to him: Go.

"Nicole?" he called. The woman didn't hear. "Nicole?"

The woman turned. She was older, in her thirties now, and pregnant, but still Nicole. "Martin?" She said it as she always had, the French way, final *n* vanishing. Then she screamed, and they embraced, and soon she was introducing her daughters Joëlle and Marie to Martin, and Martin was introducing Claire to Nicole, and the next thing Martin and Claire knew there was a dinner in their honor: a bounty of bread and bright tomatoes, cheeses and cracked olives, crustaceans in a garlicky broth and bottles of local wine, all arranged on a long oak table in a courtyard full of trees and children. *"Vendredi matin,"* Nicole's daughters were now singing, *"l'empereur, sa femme, et le petit prince . . ."*

At first Martin kept insisting that Nicole not go to any trouble, but it was easier, she told him, simply to surrender. Easier for him, because she was going to make a fuss whether he wanted one or not, and easier for her, because once word began to spread about the visiting Americans, her family and neighbors were going to be stopping by for a look anyway.

So they surrendered. Martin and Claire sat at the table as if it were their wedding day, receiving the good wishes of old women and applauding the acrobatics of children. The only time Nicole or Martin acknowledged what had happened between them so many years earlier, and what had perhaps hastened her return to Lourmarin, was in the late afternoon, when a man appeared in a doorway of the courtyard, wiping his hands on a pair of gray overalls, looking bewildered by the celebration that somehow had sprung up since he'd left for work at the garage this morning. Nicole got up from the table and went to him, but first she paused at Martin's ear.

"Thierry," she whispered. "He does not know about you."

Martin hadn't known what to expect here; he still didn't know what he wanted from this visit. At some level, he supposed, it was to show Nicole that her peculiar apprentice Martin was turning out well—well enough, anyway. That his curiosity about cooking had blossomed, and so had his interest in a woman named Claire. And if it was, in fact, Nicole's blessing he wanted, Martin more than got it. At the end of the evening, as a small band of nieces and nephews and two Americans strolled down the street to Nicole's parents' house, where Claire and Martin had agreed they would spend the night (it was useless to argue) before driving off first thing in the morning, Nicole squeezed Martin's arm and said, "She is really quite charming."

Several steps ahead, Claire was holding Joëlle's hand and trying to teach the younger girl how to skip.

"Yes," said Martin.

"And your father?"

Martin gestured with his hands. "He's not so charming."

Nicole laughed. "What does he think?"

"What you might expect."

"And you do not care?" she asked. Martin shook his head. "No?" she said.

Martin looked at her. "You don't believe me?" Nicole offered a small shrug that might have meant anything. "Tell me," he said.

"I think," said Nicole, "it does not matter what I think."

"You're wrong. It matters a great deal to me what you think," Martin said, and as soon as he had spoken he knew it to be true. "That's why I'm here," he continued. "To find out what you think."

Nicole was looking on ahead. Her husband, Thierry, was carrying the older girl on his shoulders. "Boop, boop, boop," Martin heard him singing.

"Are you happy with him?" Martin asked.

After a moment, she nodded. "He is a good father."

Like her earlier shrug this, too, might have meant anything. Martin wondered whether to pursue the question, then realized that in a way he already knew the answer: Thierry seemed to be a kind man, but he was not a man in whom a wife could confide an indiscretion with an American boy nearly half her age.

Martin and Nicole walked a few more steps in silence, and then they were in front of her parents' doorway, and the moving band of strollers slowed. There were embraces all around, double kisses, handshakes, words of thanks, promises to see one another sometime soon. Joëlle continued skipping ahead down the little street, stepping on and off the curb. Claire circled back to Martin, and he placed an arm around her shoulder.

"I think I've taught your daughter a new trick," Claire said to Nicole.

"How to run away," said Martin.

"It will happen sooner or later," Nicole said, and they all laughed. Then she turned to Martin and said, "Let me ask you something."

He felt his smile hold fast, and he became aware of how closely she was watching him. It was she who had always been the person in the house who understood him, who encouraged him, who called him in to the kitchen while his parents slept, who saw in him the potential to become something greater than the lord of the greatest hat empire in all of upstate New York. "What is it?" Martin asked.

"You are going back to Paris?"

"Sooner or later," said Martin. "We're going to Italy first, I think. Claire needs to get a few pointers from Michelangelo." At this, Claire poked him lightly.

"When you are done with Italy, go to Ireland," said Nicole. "See a friend of mine. He is the chef in a restaurant in a castle. If you are serious—"

"A castle?" said Claire.

"—about becoming a chef, about someday running your own restaurant, you will do this. Yes?" And she borrowed a pen from Martin and wrote something on a slip of pa-

per, which she handed to him. Nicole examined him a moment longer, held him
there with her gaze, then released him. She
turned to her mother and father and said
good night, called to her daughter to come
back, and then led her family up the winding
street to their home, both daughters hanging
on her arms. She was trudging back up the
hill precisely as Martin had first seen her doing this afternoon, as she no doubt did every
day, as she might have been doing right
now anyway, even if he hadn't visited, just
as if he'd never been here. And Martin
watched her go, into the night, until she was
gone.

CHAPTER SIX

In Italy, they walked. They walked under the arcade off the Piazza del Campo in Siena, pretending not to notice the unbroken stares of the men who suddenly appeared in the shop doorways at dusk, smoking. They walked through the back streets of Venice, ignoring the cries of the gondoliers who wanted to ferry them to sunny spots populated entirely by tourists, preferring instead to lose themselves along dark paths lined with distantly crying infants and hanging laundry. They walked the cool marble corridors of the Uffizi in Florence, their passage from gallery to gallery punctuated only by the repetitive clicks of their heels and the occasional, astonished "Oh." Maybe because of all the walking, they quickly adopted the custom of eating a large midday meal before retiring for a good part of the afternoon, returning to their hotel room from whatever distant quarter of whichever city they happened to be in, there to nap like newborns. And then, when they woke, they walked.

"Had enough?" Martin asked Claire one afternoon in Florence, walking back down the hill from the Pitti Palace.

"No," she answered quickly. Then, "Yes. Never." She hugged herself and lifted her head toward the rust-colored rooftops of the city on the other side of the river. "I'll never have enough time to see it all. I'd practically have to be immortal."

"That's true," he said, their pace picking up now, their steps quickening as they neared the bottom of the hill. "The trick is to know when to stop."

But it was difficult for Claire to imagine wanting to stop, to imagine calling a voluntary halt to the endless procession of rich food and rich art that spread out before them. This was what she'd wanted to do for years. No, that wasn't quite true. This life she found herself leading now hadn't even been a wish. It was more an idle thought, a daydream she'd barely indulged: Europe, the unthinking answer to the question of where would she like to go if she could go anywhere in the world. But now it was real, and its vividness stopped her at every turn: frescoes in chapels, tapestries in churches, paintings in galleries, sculptures in gardens. Faced with one more hill, she climbed; with one more bridge, she crossed. How could she not? Her new Italian walking shoes were made of sturdy, resilient cowhide, and who knew what treasure might be waiting on the other side?

Yet she would have to stop. As difficult as it was to imagine their travels ever coming to an end, it was equally difficult to imagine being able to go on like this much longer. It wasn't just the walking, though the liquid-limbed fatigue at the end of the day was an unfamiliar and unpleasant experience for Claire. And it was more than homesickness, or the private embarrassment she might feel at not being able to recognize the style of a particular artist, or remember even in what century he had lived. The weariness that was overtaking them now was something new. It was the momentum of their trip, its acceleration and accumulation, and Claire was the one who was going to have to say, "Enough."

Martin wouldn't; she knew that. Paris, perhaps, had been his. Lourmarin, definitely. But Italy was all Claire's. Martin could leave her in front of a triptych or sculpture, go out for a cappuccino, pick up a copy of the *International Herald Tribune,* and come back to find her in the exact position he'd left her. He amused himself with simple trattoria fare; he wolfed down bowls of spaghetti *con burro* with a fork and soupspoon, his face shining with butter; he learned to distinguish among the olive oils of various regions—the green ones, the gold ones, the ones swirling with sediment; he insisted they stop at a different gelato vendor every evening on the long walk back to the small, elegant Hotel Paolo e Francesca, near the Duomo. Sometimes Martin might gently question her, nudge her, ask her if she'd had enough yet—not rushing her, he'd emphasize, just asking—and sometimes Claire would concede that she had. But then she would ask if he would mind too much if they stayed just a little longer, another day, two at the *most*. Martin's smile at these moments wasn't exactly indulgent; once, Claire made the mistake of calling it that.

"I'm not *indulging* you," Martin corrected her. They were walking past yet another series of early Renaissance crucifixions, trying to remember where to turn for the gallery that housed Michelangelo's *David*. "I don't indulge you. I can't imagine wanting to spend time with anyone I would need to indulge."

"But sometimes I feel like it actually hurts to see so much art," she said. "My eyes hurt. My head hurts. My teeth actually hurt."

"And then," Martin said.

"Right. Exactly. And then I see something I've never seen before and the pain goes away and I forget everything else in the world."

"Even me."

"Even you," she admitted. "Is that okay?"

"If I'm going to lose you to someone," Martin said, "it may as well be Michelangelo."

And then they turned a corner, found the statue *David,* and after a minute Martin invisibly withdrew, knowing that this was the right thing to do. She needed to be alone here; she'd never explicitly said it, but he knew it was the case.

Several times Claire had visited *David*. It was almost a cliché, her allegiance to this particular work of all the masterpieces in Florence. She didn't come here and keep coming here just because she wanted to learn from the master. This wasn't a matter of looking harder. It was true that the more she looked, the more she learned; but this was true of most any work of art. What Claire hoped to get here, standing in this airy gallery far below the gentle curvature of a dome, several yards from the museum guards who now nodded to her each day because she had become a familiar face, was something more than an education.

When she looked at the *David*, she thought of herself. At first Claire tried to dismiss the association outright: how immodest to compare yourself with *David,* symbol of physical perfection. Yet it made a kind of sense. What Claire saw wasn't just his nakedness. In David's even gaze and the casual angle of his ankle, what Claire found was an acceptance of nakedness: the shrugging entitlement, the vague awareness of the natural gifts of being young. Sometimes, easing herself down from the precarious height of a four-poster hotel bed, Claire would catch sight of her own naked body in a full-length hotel dressing mirror, and the simple fact of what she saw then, imperfect though it was, thrilled her in the same way that *David* did.

But most of all what the *David* reminded her of, of course, was Martin. When he returned to the gallery this afternoon, he found Claire staring up at the *David* exactly where he'd left her half an hour earlier. He'd been at lunch somewhere; there was still a slight gleam of oil on the corner of his mouth. She glanced at Martin, then took his arm, running her hand up the sleeve of his cotton summer shirt, touching hair, then muscle.

They skipped the gelato that evening. When they got back to the Hotel Paolo e Francesca, Claire pinned Martin to the bed, climbing on top of him with a new need that, if she'd thought about it, might have alarmed her. So she didn't think about it. Instead, she saw it through, and when it had passed, Claire slid off Martin, who was still startled but happy, then lay beside him on the bed, and said, "Enough."

* * *

In Ireland, a sedan from the hotel met them at the train station in Galway, and half an hour later they were pulling up the long drive through the grounds leading to the front gate of Thetford Castle, a vast but uncomplicated kingdom.

After the narrow cobblestone streets of Italy, Claire and Martin luxuriated in long, aimless walks across seemingly endless Irish fields. At the hotel restaurant at Thetford, Martin's choice of food remained consistent. Every day he sampled a different preparation of the same fish, the ubiquitous Irish salmon that was as plentiful here as zucchini was in the summertime in Longwood Falls. The salmon had been plucked that very day from the packed river that ran through the property, and he ate it smoked, on toast, with capers and lemon; baked with butter and dill; steamed in parchment with tomato and onion. And although the halls of Thetford Castle housed the occasional suit of armor or heraldic crest, Claire found it oddly relieving not to have to wonder which door might be hiding a collection of masterpieces stacked, like bread in a bakery, with offhand indifference.

The second day at Thetford, Martin worked up the nerve to introduce himself to the chef, a tall, sandy-haired Englishman named Duncan Lear, who at first regarded the appearance of a customer in his kitchen with deep apprehension. When Martin mentioned their mutual friend, the French cook Nicole, however, Duncan's mood lightened. And when Martin said that one day he hoped to open a restaurant of his own, Duncan invited him to have a look around. Martin slowly circulated among the assistants variously boning, cutting, stirring, calling out orders, and recoiling from steam.

"The cook's tour," Duncan said, but Martin didn't offer even a polite smile. He was lost among the washtub-size pots hanging at eye level, running his hand along the blackened bottom of a cauldron that was used to cook God knows what.

"Look," Duncan said, realizing how entranced Martin was, and how serious, "if you like, you can come back here one day and try your hand at something. We could always use help in the kitchen; it's sort of a madhouse. How long are you staying at the hotel?"

Martin shrugged. "How long do I have?"

Duncan laughed a little, then sobered. "It's real work, you know. It's not easy. It's not all fun and food."

"I know. I don't expect it to be."

Duncan regarded him. "All right, then. Come by tomorrow after lunch. We'll plan something together for the dinner menu."

The following afternoon, Martin lingered with Claire at a corner table in the restaurant, draining cups of coffee, waiting for the last of the other diners to clear out. "Come on, come on," Martin whispered, eyeing the stylish Dutch couple across the room sharing a slab of dense chocolate cake. Their forks were approaching from opposite sides of the plate, and out of either politeness or the desire to make a heavenly dessert last longer, they were taking uniformly small helpings of cake.

"They're doing it on purpose," Martin said, and Claire shushed him.

When at last the chic chocolate cake couple had finished and signed their bill and risen to leave, Claire said, "Well, this is it."

"Wish me luck," he said.

"You won't need it," she answered. "What do you say to wish a chef luck, anyway? 'Break an egg'?"

"Good. Very good," said Martin. "This is what I'm going to be thinking about all afternoon now. Your horrible pun is going to haunt me, somehow seeping like a bad taste into the food, and if I fail in my first day as a professional but unpaid kitchen worker, it'll be all your fault."

"Martin?" she said as he rose to leave. He stopped, turned to Claire. "Good luck."

He hadn't realized how hot the kitchen of a restaurant was, although, looking around him at all the other workers, nobody else seemed particularly affected by the heat. Martin kept wiping his forehead and neck throughout the afternoon, and as all the ovens were lit in anticipation of the approaching dinner hour, the heat became suffocating.

"You all right?" Duncan asked, and Martin nodded and said he was.

"Good, then," said the chef, distracted by a waiter asking him a question on the other side of the huge, gleaming room. "Why don't you go help out with the chopping, then?"

"The chopping" turned out to be an endless session devoted to potatoes, chicken breasts, and, especially, scallions. Mountains of scallions, long and slender and bulbous at the tip, scallions that lay across the countertop like hanks of long green hair. Knives flashed; when one became the slightest bit dull, a whetstone was produced, and the knife was dragged along it, making a sound that set Martin's teeth on edge. Of course, it was only a matter of an hour or so before he cut himself on a just-sharpened blade, an event that seemed commonplace to the rest of the staff, although the amount of blood was, at first, slightly alarming to Martin. Where was Claire to take care of him, as she had done the day of his black eye in the gazebo? Someone tossed him an adhesive bandage, and a moment later someone else gave him a new pile of potatoes and told him to get started.

But after all the chopping was through, Duncan called him over to a cooler part of the kitchen, near the refrigerators, and sat with him for a while to discuss the week's menus. Duncan spoke eloquently about the different foods, about how he arrived at his choices, and Martin found himself paying attention in a way he had rarely done even in class at Princeton.

"Why don't you try to come up with a dinner?" Duncan asked. "Remember, think salmon." And with a little encouragement Martin mumbled a few new ideas, some of which Duncan lightly mocked, others which he commended. The next night, Duncan included two of Martin's suggestions on the dinner menu.

Martin was thrilled, overexcited; when he came back to the suite late that night, Claire was asleep in the huge bed that looked out over the lawn and, slightly farther, a lake. She woke up then, lightly sniffing the air. "Scallions?" she said, and then she went right back to sleep.

For three days and nights, Martin Rayfiel worked in the kitchen at Thetford. It made the manager of the hotel nervous that one of the paying guests should be willingly exerting himself in this way, but Duncan Lear reassured the manager that this was what Martin wanted, that this was only adding to his stay at the castle. "Perhaps I should put all my guests to work," said the manager. "The women could become chambermaids." But he didn't stop Martin from working in the kitchen. Martin even celebrated his twenty-first birthday there. The entire staff surprised him while he was stewing a chicken. They gathered around him, singing in harmony. He was legally grown and could collect his inheritance now, which was a good thing, since the money from the sale of the family crest was rapidly diminishing.

Each day while he worked, Claire took a sketch pad and wandered the grounds until she found the one thing she'd decided to draw, in hopes of turning the sketch into a sculpture sometime: an old horse drinking water from a trough. Every afternoon she came back to this same spot and sketched until the tin of charcoal she had bought in Italy had been reduced to pieces as tiny as little pebbles, Claire's fingertips now black.

She would need to find some more charcoal somewhere; maybe the man at the front desk would know where she could buy some. Claire stood and began to walk back toward the castle. The day was utterly silent, and as the path she was walking on broke out into the main open field, she looked up and saw a person walking way ahead in the distance. It was Martin. At first Claire was surprised that he wasn't in the kitchen, but then, as she looked at him, she became more than surprised. She was worried.

There was something about the way he was walking—his shoulders hunched, his head down—that was very uncharacteristic. It was as though he had been pacing the field. Claire lifted a hand to wave to him, but he seemed not to see.

By the time she got back to the castle, he was sitting on the edge of their bed. The look in his eyes when he finally raised his face toward Claire was something she'd never seen there before. "Are you okay?" she asked, the question pointless, because she already knew the answer.

He paused for a long moment before he spoke. "I have bad news," he finally said. "I'll make it simple. The money is gone."

"Oh," Claire said. She slid next to him on the edge of the bed before she even had a chance to try to understand what he was saying. "What do you mean?" she asked him. "I don't understand."

"That's it. It's gone. My inheritance. All of it."

She heard him this time, but his words still seemed to be taking a while to get to her, as if they were arriving from a great distance. He was explaining to her that now that he was twenty-one he thought he'd surprise her, that he had walked into Cong, the town on the other side of the property line, and stopped at a bank and tried to have the money from his inheritance wired there. When he was done talking, he fell silent, miserably. Claire reached for his hand and took it in hers. "But this is impossible," she said. "That's your money."

"With my father," Martin reminded her, "nothing is impossible."

"But I don't understand. It *is* your money, isn't it?"

"Yes, it is. Was."

"So he can't do that," she said.

"Claire, he *did* it. He took it back."

"But that's impossible—" Claire started to say again, but Martin cut her off. "Would you please stop saying 'it's impossible, it's impossible,' because it's not. It's obviously not impossible, because it just happened."

It was the first time Martin had raised his voice to Claire, ever. And they both understood at once that it was no coincidence it had come within moments of discovering that their entire future had changed. The touch of their hands suddenly seemed too much, and wordlessly they allowed them to slide apart.

"All right," Claire said, softly. "Not impossible, then. Illegal."

"And immoral, too," Martin answered, just as softly, "but I don't think my father cares about either of those concerns."

"But isn't there something you can do?" she asked. She had grown up thinking that there was always something that *could be* done. If a friend made you unhappy, you spent less time with that friend. If you were untalented at arithmetic, you studied harder before the next test. It was a naive attitude, she saw now, and she was embarrassed. The world of Ash Rayfiel, its finances and father-son antagonism, was beyond her frame of reference.

"Probably," Martin said. "I could sue him, I guess. Report him to the police. Nothing I *would* do."

"So what *will* you do?"

"Nothing."

Claire crossed her legs, folded her hands on her lap. "Is that best?" she asked, her voice sounding prim, like her mother's.

"It's wisest, I think."

"You've thought this through already," Claire said.

"On the walk back from Cong. A slow walk."

"I saw you. I waved."

"Did you? I'm sorry. I didn't notice. That must have been when I was looking at the lake. I was thinking what it would be like never to see it again."

They each had something they needed to do then. Martin had raised his voice, and now it was up to him to take Claire's hand back, or at least to make the effort. For her part, Claire knew that Martin could never say what he really thought about the money—the loss of the money—not unless she said it first.

Martin reached for Claire's hand, and Claire reached back and said to him in a quiet voice, "You know, the money doesn't matter."

Claire waited, then she stood and paced across the beautiful room to the window. Lough Corrib was out there, a lake by a castle in Ireland, a lake she and Martin had slept over, that she had sketched, that— Martin was right—neither of them might ever see again. Could it really be starting so soon, when they were still only twenty-one years old: a litany of good-byes to favorite places?

"No more expensive boutiques," she heard Martin saying behind her. "No more going somewhere on a whim. No more apple-green Chanel suits."

"I never needed any of that," Claire answered. "And by the way, the ridiculous suit was your idea. You insisted."

"I know," he said. "But how can you go back to the life you had before without resenting me a little bit for it? Not for losing the money. But for showing you what money could do."

"My mother used to have a name for it when I'd start feeling sorry for myself," Claire said. "She'd say, 'Poor Me is here again. Who invited her over, Claire? Was it you? Go home, Poor Me, go home.' "

"Well, we won't be poor, anyway," Martin said. "We'll just be . . . *normal.* People with jobs, and rent to pay."

"I think, in a strange way, it might be better this way," said Claire. "Otherwise, don't you think we'd become spoiled—sort of horrible? And some part of ourselves would always wonder, Did we do that? Was that us? Did I open that restaurant? Did I make that sculpture and sell it to that gallery? Or was it really just the money all along?"

"So now we'll know," Martin said.

"Now," Claire echoed, "we'll know."

In its own way, the grounds of Thetford Castle and the nearby community of Cong were as much a small town as Longwood Falls, and maybe even smaller. News traveled fast, and there were no secrets. By the time Martin appeared at the reception desk that evening and asked to speak to the manager, he knew from the muted response and averted eyes of the usually talkative staff that word was out: the American couple were going broke and would have to make an early departure. Martin quietly settled his account, and the following morning, as he was carrying their bags out the front door to the car waiting to take them back to Galway, Duncan Lear approached him, already dressed in his chef's whites for another day in that big, overheated kitchen.

"Sorry," he said to Martin. "Heard you'd be leaving us. Let me give you a hand with that." He took a bag from Martin and carried it out the door. After the two men had loaded the bags in the back of the car, Duncan pulled Martin aside, onto the lawn behind the fountain where a stone mermaid stood. Nobody could possibly overhear them here, but Duncan still glanced around nervously.

"I haven't made this public," Duncan said, "so obviously it's just between us. But I'm giving notice next week. I've gotten an offer to work in a restaurant in London. Fellow I know opened it earlier this year, and it hasn't quite hit its stride yet. It's in a very desirable neighborhood. Kensington. You know the area?"

Martin nodded. He had stayed at a hotel in Kensington with his parents and nanny, many years earlier. There was a book, too, a sequel to *Peter Pan* called *Peter Pan in Kensington Gardens,* which Martin had read after that trip. The area was beautiful, the gardens lush and sprawling.

"Would you like to come work for me there? I've got to put together a staff rather quickly. I hope you're not offended at the notion," Duncan continued quickly. "It's just that we heard your news, and I wanted to be of some help." He paused. "You've got a real talent," he said. "I think you might have a future in cooking. If that's what you want. Although," he added, "you might want to brush up on your knife skills a little."

So while they had thought they would be leaving the castle with a feeling of loss and aimlessness, Claire and Martin ended up leaving with something much different: an offer. The money wouldn't be much, Duncan had warned, but he could provide Claire and Martin with the use of a small flat above the restaurant, at a very reasonable rent in an otherwise unreasonably expensive neighborhood.

Martin and Claire spent a few nights in a cheap student hostel in London, and then Martin started his job the following week, as soon as Duncan arrived in the city. The restaurant, known only by its address, 17 Dobson Mews, was small and pretty, and its kitchen offered steel counters, rows of burners on the stoves, and, though food rationing was still in effect in England, a supply of very interesting ingredients.

That first day in the restaurant, Martin worked and worked, helping Duncan set up, and at night, he and Claire went to bed in their new flat upstairs. The rooms were furnished, though not particularly nicely. There was a nondescript living room with a brown nubby sofa and chairs, and a small no-frills bathroom. The only piece of furniture they liked was the curved black teak sleigh bed. But the one true luxury of the flat was the large back room, which was flooded with light. Claire could use it as a studio, Martin suggested as they lay in bed. "At least for now," he added. "When we have children, I'm afraid you'll have to turn the room over to them."

"Children," she said. "We're not even married."

He turned to her in the sleigh bed, which creaked slightly beneath them. It seemed that this bed might lift off the ground and take them somewhere, anywhere; it seemed to have magical properties. No, Martin corrected himself, it was their *life* that had these properties. He was enormously fortunate in having Claire, and the kind of work he loved, in a city that they hadn't yet explored. But best of all, they were finally settling down. It was starting: the part where they didn't need to keep checking train schedules or signing hotel registers or waking up in the night and wondering where they were. The part where they stayed in one place, and where they turned it into their own, so that after a while they developed an attachment to it, a need to be here.

"I think," he said carefully, "that we ought to think about getting married then, don't you?"

Both of them were always thinking about marriage, of course, but they had been on the move constantly, living in various unfamiliar places, and it wouldn't have seemed natural. But now here they were, Martin settling into his dream job, Claire beginning sculpture classes at the Tate with a wonderful, idiosyncratic teacher, the two of them starting from scratch in an appealing flat. They would get married within the next few weeks, they decided.

When they broached the subject with Duncan, he insisted they hold the ceremony at the restaurant. "Invite anyone you like," the chef said, magnanimously.

"But we don't know anyone in London," said Claire.

"Well," Duncan said, "invite me."

That night, after the end of another long day, Claire turned to Martin and said, "Oh, my God."

"What is it?" he asked.

"I just realized," she said. "Our children are going to have British accents."

Claire wasn't used to the sound of the buzzer on the front door of the flat. Because they still had very few friends here, almost no one ever pressed the green metal bell beside the door frame. Once, a man had come by delivering eggs to the restaurant and had rung the wrong buzzer, but that was it. So when the buzzer rang one morning, after Claire and Martin had been living their newly settled life upstairs at 17 Dobson Mews for two weeks, Claire jumped. She had been sitting and making a sketch for a sculpture she wanted to do in her class at the Tate that afternoon. The sound was sharp, unfriendly: a long, demanding bleat.

She opened the door. A Western Union messenger was standing on the top step, speaking her name and handing forward an envelope. The telegram read:

MOTHER VERY ILL STOP COME HOME STOP
LOVE MARGARET

She felt something twist slightly inside her, and a sudden panic threatened to over-

take her. She had barely been thinking
about her mother and father, and now look
what had happened. Since she had been in
Europe, she'd dutifully written home with ad-
dresses where she could be reached in an
emergency, though she'd never given it any
real thought. But now she understood she
had reached the day that anyone choosing
to live abroad for any period remotely resembling forever sooner or later must face.
She would have to go to the States tomorrow; they had very little money, but would
need to scrape enough together to cover her
airfare. Slowly, Claire went downstairs to the
restaurant. Martin was sitting with three
other men at a table in the back, snapping
green beans.

"The wedding. We'll have to wait a little
while," she said to him, after she'd shown
him the telegram.

"That's not important," he said.

"Of course it is."

"I'm just so sorry to hear this, Claire," he
said. "I should come with you. I mean, I
should be with you."

"No, you should be here," she answered.
"They need you here. And if *I* need you, I'll
send for you. I swear."

"Claire—"

"It's very sweet of you to want to come with me, Martin," she said, "and I really do appreciate it. But I'll be back really soon. My God—my whole life is here. You're here. Our future children and their little accents are here. *I'm* here." She touched the starched chest of Martin's white apron. "I'm *here*," she repeated.

Claire left London on a wet autumn morning. Moments after takeoff, clouds erased her entire view of the city she had just been getting to know, and Claire found herself studying instead the droplets collecting on the outside of the window, drifting slowly in the wrong direction, seemingly defying gravity. Rain falling *up*: it was something she'd never seen before, something she couldn't have predicted, precisely the kind of thing, she suspected, that would be waiting for her in the house on Badger Street. Several times she'd tried to imagine what she might find there, but she'd come up empty. Completely blank. And the telegram was no help. Her sister's choice of the word *very*, in particular: how ill was very ill? The possibilities were endless, and therefore each fantasy about it was meaningless, and when Claire tried to imagine life in Longwood Falls she saw nothing. All she could picture now with any certainty was what she'd left behind in London. Claire leaned her forehead against the oval of the airplane window, stared into the fog, and thought, Go home, Poor Me, go home.

CHAPTER SEVEN

December 1, 1952

M.,

I noticed yesterday that the gazebo has icicles hanging from it. No one sits inside it now; the temperature is much too cold for that. Instead, we all stay inside our homes, and I suppose other people in town feel content, but all I feel is how incredibly WRONG it is not being with you.

My mother had surgery last week to remove diseased tissue from her breast (cancerous, the doctor said, although the surgery was considered a success), and now she's weak and in pain, and it's quite frightening to see her like this. The doctor told me that if she's to make a "swift" recovery, ha ha (he thought he was very clever using that word, as though he's the first person who's ever told us a *swift* joke), she will need a great deal of care, and I promised that I would be here for her.

Most of the time I sit by her bed and read to her (she likes the poems of Edna St. Vincent Millay—especially: "My candle burns at both ends . . .") or else I prepare some beef consommé or a soft-cooked egg—badly, I'm sorry to say; they would be much more delicious if you'd made them—or bring her some of the tablets that the doctor prescribed for the pain.

I'm also helping take care of my father, too; he seems anguished and forgetful now, and this morning he actually started to head for work still wearing his striped pajama top, and I had to call him back inside. I'm only sorry that I wasn't here when my mother first got sick; I have to

say I feel really guilty about that sometimes. There we were, thoughtlessly
happy and self-involved in our little London life, while she was over here suffering with cancer. My sister, Margaret,
comes over to help when she can, but
her twins are only four months old, and
it's virtually impossible for her to get
away for very long. When one twin is
sleeping, the other is wide awake and
crying, and the color of a beefsteak tomato. (Remind me, Martin, when we
have our own children, to ask God to
give them to us one at a time, not all at
once, okay?)

I miss you all the time. Please write
and tell me how 17 Dobson Mews is going. Are you good at making scones yet?
I hear it's a requirement for U.K. citizen-
ship. All my love,

Claire

December 14, 1952

Dear Claire,

I'm very sad to hear that your mother
is so weak and ill. I would send her a few
bottles of Devonshire cream, but I don't
think they would survive the journey. I

know this is a terrible time for you, and want you to know I think you are a WONDERFUL daughter!!! (Note the exclamation marks.) Please don't feel guilty; you couldn't have known she would become sick. And her illness has nothing to do with our European fling . . .

I agree that we should have our own children one after the other, but if they should be born in a litter like piglets, I wouldn't be too upset. 17 D.M. is doing even better than ever, if you can believe it. I feel that the restaurant is charmed. It seems that there's all this local talk about the "American" in the kitchen (me) who not only cooks "classic American" dishes like apple pie and macaroni and cheese, but also complicated and intricate Continental dishes. The other night we had to turn people away at the door, the dining room was so full. We were cleaning up until three in the morning, but no one seemed to mind; everyone likes being part of a success, I guess. Duncan and the entire kitchen staff send you their love. (All right, their *regards*.) Me, I send you my love . . .

Martin

Abby put down the letters, leaned back in her chair, and closed her eyes. She had finished two tapes now, and she had begun digging through the photographs of Martin and Claire all over Europe: kissing at the base of the Eiffel Tower, posed in front of the Uffizi, standing on either side of a poker-faced Beefeater at Buckingham Palace, and embracing in front of a huge, mossy stone castle in Ireland. Then had come the correspondence between Claire and Martin—letter after urgent letter bringing each other up-to-date on their separate lives. Abby wished that Claire had never gotten the telegram, that the wedding had taken place at 17 Dobson Mews as planned, that Martin and Claire had been able to stay together in London, sleeping in the sleigh bed of their small flat and starting the rest of their life together. But life, of course, rarely worked according to some plan or diagram. Claire had boarded a plane to Paris in 1952; Abby had a baby on her own in 1992. Each, in her own way, had departed.

And then, abruptly, returned. When Abby took the train back to Longwood Falls for her father's funeral, she had no way of knowing she was going home for good. If her father had groomed her, had expected her to take over the newspaper, maybe it would have been easier to walk away from it. But her father had never expected any such thing of Abby. He had seemed to appreciate the fact that she was a different person from him, someone with her own interests and a complicated inner life. When he'd bring friends or business associates by the house and they would shake her hand and ask if they were having the pleasure of meeting the future editor of the *Ledger,* Abby's father always answered from the background, "I think maybe Abby's going to be a city girl." The choice, if and when the time should come, would be Abby's, and in the end, the choice was this: return to Longwood Falls, or let the lifework of her father die with him.

Her mother didn't exactly tell Abby what to do. In fact, Helen Reston had refused to offer an opinion. But when Abby told her mother, the morning after the funeral, that she would take over the paper, her mother had seemed to breathe more easily than she had in days, as if relieved that some part of her husband, Tom, would endure after all.

Still, Abby wondered what her parents had meant to each other. Back when she had imagined that she and Sam Bachman would one day settle on the same coast and grow old together, Abby had thought she had found what her mother had not: a man who wasn't afraid to be expressive about love. But when Abby became pregnant and Sam disappeared, she realized that somehow she'd gotten it entirely wrong.

And now, even if a man did come along who seemed willing to explore what life with a thirty-five-year-old single mother of one might be like, Abby couldn't bear the thought of starting over, or, more to the point, ending *up*—after she'd opened herself in ways she'd never thought possible—alone again.

One weekend back in New York City, Miranda had spiked an extremely high fever and lost all her energy, and Abby had bundled her into a taxi and taken her to the covering pediatrician, a young, shaggy doctor she'd never heard of. But Nick Kelleher was gentle, prescribing a pink antibiotic and calming child and mother alike. He'd called that Monday to see how Miranda was doing, and then he'd called Tuesday to see how Abby was doing, and he'd kept calling—in

New York City, then up here, first just to chat a little, but then offering to come up and visit, saying he occasionally had a weekend off, and he really liked the landscape of up-state New York, and was there a decent place in the area where he could stay? Abby, of course, always had brilliant, unas-sailable excuses why she couldn't see him, and the wonder of it was that she hadn't scared him off by now. It wasn't fair; it wasn't right. But it was all she could do.

Abby placed her elbows on her desk and rubbed her eyes. Then she poured herself a new glass of wine and reached toward the tape player, curious to see how Claire was faring in her own return to Longwood Falls.

Claire had moved back into her parents' house on Badger Street to help her mother, but she no longer slept in her childhood bed-room. That room now belonged to Maureen Swift, who needed her own bed at night because she often tossed and turned for hours. Claire slept on a folding cot in the living room, and when she heard her mother mumbling or crying in the night she would bring her another pain tablet or a washcloth dipped in cool water.

At first, her mother had been shocked to see her when she arrived home from Europe. "Well, what did you expect?" Claire had said to her. "When I got the telegram from Margaret, I couldn't just stay there in England. I had to come home."

"But I told Margaret not to trouble you," her mother had said in her muted voice, a hint of chill coming through. "I told her that you had your own life now—you and Martin—and that it was the way you wanted it."

The words hurt, even though they hadn't been meant to; they were a paraphrase of what Claire herself had written in the note to her parents that she had propped up on the kitchen table before she left. She was twenty-one years old and was entitled to her own life, but now, with her mother suddenly so sick, the situation had become more complex, and all the terms seemed to have changed. Claire's life was waiting for her in London, but she couldn't go and join it yet. She wanted to be with Martin—could think of nothing else, when she wasn't worrying about her mother—but it wasn't really a choice. Despite the difficulties between Claire and her mother, she would stay in Longwood Falls and take care of her, as her mother had taken care of Claire when she was a baby.

Sometimes, over the weeks, Maureen Swift felt just fine for an hour or two, and during those periods Claire would play card games with her, the two women sitting at the kitchen table and slapping down cards in a surprisingly lively game of hearts or blackjack. Claire would tune the radio that sat on the kitchen window to a popular music station, and let "Mood Indigo" and "I've Got You under My Skin" drift into the room like a light wind. They talked, mother and daughter, in a way they had never talked before. She found herself speaking at length about Martin.

"I can't say I approve of it," Maureen Swift said after a while. "The two of you going off together like that, not being married or anything. So please don't ask me to."

"I won't," Claire said softly. "But if it makes a difference, we're planning on getting married, you know. As soon as I go back to London." These words seemed to upset Maureen, and Claire realized she had been insensitive. Her mother would not want her to go back to London, of course; she would want her to stay nearby, even though she wouldn't say so. "You know," Claire continued, "I'm not running away. I'm just going back there to be with him. It's become our home. He's found a wonderful job there—the kind of job he's always wanted, to his absolute amazement—and we've got a little flat upstairs with a sunny room in back where I can sculpt. I've been taking classes at the Tate, with the most dynamic teacher, Mr. Paley. He came over to me after class the other day and said that he actually thinks I have real talent."

Her mother turned, and Claire could see the physical pain she was once again feeling, but something more, too. "You know, Claire," she said, "I wouldn't have chosen this life for you, God only knows, but since it's there and it isn't going to go away, I have to say that I'm glad he makes you happy. But are you sure you want to be so far away from everything?"

"No," Claire said, after a moment.

They sat in silence then, slapping down cards and drinking the hot cider that Claire had mulled from one of Martin's recipes. The small kitchen smelled of cloves and toasted orange rind, a perfume that made everything slightly more bearable. Finally her mother put down her cards and said, "I know why you went with him. I didn't used to understand, but now I do."

"Oh?" was all Claire could say.

"I used to think you were just running away from us," said Maureen Swift. "From our family, from the fact that we didn't have a lot of money, or many things to offer you. I guess my feelings were hurt, knowing that you would choose him over us." She took a deep breath, something inside her causing her a new rush of pain. "But I see you now," she went on, "and I see that you're different. You went with him so that you could change. It would have been impossible for you to do it here. Now your sister, Margaret, she was perfectly happy to marry Larry Benton and move into a house three streets away from us and work as a doctor's receptionist and then have those darling twins. But you—that wasn't the path you were taking, was it?"

"No," said Claire softly.

"I'll never be pleased about it," her mother went on, "but you did it, and now you're different, and what can I say?"

Her mother was right; she was different. It had happened in slow, ineffable ways, slipping over her at night while she slept or made love with Martin. The lovemaking was a part of it, certainly, for in the months that they had been together in Europe she had been able to feel a true sense of privacy for the first time ever. In the sleigh bed with him in the flat in Kensington, touching each other with hands, mouths—it had only intensified.

But it was everything else, too. The world of two they had created in bed at night had spread, inevitably, throughout everything they did. In the end, they needed very little. They had lived well in the hotels and restaurants of Europe, and then they had lived not as well in a London flat, but the drastic reduction in money hadn't changed anything, really. Claire didn't miss the opulence of their early days in Europe, the thick towels, the translucent china, the maids slipping silently in and out of rooms; it had begun to be too much. Even without any money she could be open with him, she could be free. When she was a girl growing up in Longwood Falls, Claire had been many things, but she certainly hadn't been free.

January 5, 1953

Dear Martin,
The New Year came and went, and I

barely noticed. I had hoped that my mother would be feeling better by now, but in fact she's not. The doctor is concerned, and yesterday we all traveled to the hospital in Albany for some further tests. I'll let you know when we get the results. I wish I could count the days until we can be together, except I don't have a specific number to count down from. I can still smell you and hear your voice. Sometimes I wake up on this little cot in the living room, confused for a second, imagining that you're beside me. But of course you never are.

Claire

January 15, 1953

Darling C.,

I'm so sorry that things don't seem to be improving. I will cross my fingers about your mother's test results. Today I made a vanilla cake for Duncan that was so rich and intense it reminded me of being with you. (Does that embarrass you? Hope not.) I won't save you a piece, for I don't think you're coming home this week. Duncan asked if I might consider staying on here *permanently*—really turn-

ing this restaurant into my own place
when he leaves, which, he hinted, might
be sooner rather than later. He has this
fantasy of opening up another restaurant—
something bigger and more casual—in
the southwest of England, maybe Exeter.
But I told him, of course, that I'd have to
talk to you. Do you think London would
be a place you'd be happy living forever?
The back room of the flat is yours forever
to work in, and we could take frequent
trips to France and Spain and to Italy,
whenever you need another heavy dose
of that naked statue *David* that gets you
so excited. . . . Give it some thought
when you have a moment, sweetheart,
though I know you're so worried. I'm
praying that the tests come out well. I
love you.

                                        Martin

                              January 17, 1953
Dear Martin,
   I decided not to wait for your letter to
arrive before I answered. I needed to
write to you today to let you know what's
going on. My mother's test results came
back, and they weren't good. It seems

that the cancer has returned, and now there is nothing more that can be done for her. The doctor said he will try to make her comfortable, which essentially means plying her with a ton of morphine. She isn't herself anymore but has gone into some strange new state, as though she's in a dream. I'm so sad to think I will never have my mother back, and that there is no way to make her better. My poor father doesn't know what to do with himself. He just sits by her side and talks to her quietly about things that happened a long time ago, when they were young. When he is sure she's asleep, he lets himself cry.

PLEASE don't do anything dumb like flying here. I know how incredibly busy you are at the restaurant, not to mention the fact that we can't afford the airfare, and that really, I'm doing fine.

Love,
Claire

CLAIRE STOP I AM FLYING OVER IMMEDI-ATELY DESPITE WHAT YOU SAY STOP MEET ME AT GAZEBO TOMORROW MORNING STOP MARTIN

Martin arrived at the gazebo rumpled and unshaven from the long flight out of London and then the long train ride up from New York City, but he didn't care how he looked. Everyone in Longwood Falls thought he was wild, anyway; now he simply looked the part. He stepped off the train and strode through town, feeling a strange sensation at being back here after so many months. Was it possible that the place had grown smaller, or had the vast patchwork expanse of Europe made this town seem like a miniature? He felt nostalgia ripple across him, although most of the feeling was connected to Claire; Longwood Falls had had the most meaning for him in terms of his relationship with her. He thought: here is the path we used to walk, and down the road a few miles is our motel, and over this way is the tree we sat under. And, of course, he thought: there is our gazebo.

And there it was, with Claire inside it. This time she wasn't smiling. Her expression was tight, controlled. She stood when he walked up the shallow steps. "I told you not to come," she said.

"I guess I forgot. And besides, how could I leave you here alone?"

"But the restaurant—" she began.

"Oh, damn the restaurant," Martin said. "This isn't about that."

Claire regarded him with a tired expression. He knew that she barely slept anymore, that all she did was help take care of her mother and father and run the household. "I don't need to be taken care of, Martin," she said. "I don't need to be babied."

"Of course you do," he said. "Everyone does sometimes."

"No," she insisted. "I've gotten into this other mode, this caretaking mode. My mother has needed *me,* so I've made myself available. And my father needs me, too."

"I'm not going to force myself on you," he said evenly. "I just want to help make things easier, if that's possible. Please," he said, "why don't you let me help you a little." Then he came forward and held his arms out to her. There was a pause, as though she was deciding what to do, and then she stepped forward into his arms, as though she and Martin were about to start dancing.

"By the way, you smell terrible," Claire said. "And your beard is like sandpaper."

"I'll take a bath and shave as soon as I can," he said. "I'm staying at the Lookout—

room eighteen, of course. But first," he added, "can I come home with you to your parents' house?"

She drew back and looked at him. "I doubt that they'd want to see you, Martin." She paused. "I mean, you're not the enemy," she said, "but they're not thrilled, either. I guess they figure if I want to make an eccentric, living-in-sin life for myself on another continent with an inappropriate man," Claire said, "there's nothing they can do about it. So they've accepted it. Or they've tried, anyway."

"So let me come to the house," Martin said.

Claire looked at him again. "All right," she said. "You can come."

That evening he returned to Badger Street and stood in the Swifts' tiny kitchen, preparing a pot of vegetable soup for Claire's mother. He used the best ingredients he could find at short notice, adding some herbs that he'd heard bore healing properties, and then pureeing it all so that it was smooth as baby's gruel. Maureen, who hadn't kept any food down in days, was somehow able to eat a small bowl of his soup. At first, when Martin walked through the door, both Claire's parents were suspicious and stiff, but after a while, when Martin had quietly commandeered the kitchen and set to work, they softened somewhat.

He came every morning and quietly cooked for Claire's mother, preparing dishes that were identically smooth in texture but quite different from one another in taste: soups; cereals; purees of beet, parsnip, sweet potato, leek. And he made his own ice cream for the family too. Martin spent hours in the small, inadequate kitchen, cooking for Claire's mother, a woman who had never liked him or what he had done with her daughter, and at the end of the day he went back to the Lookout Motel and quickly fell asleep alone in the sagging bed.

One afternoon at the end of March, Maureen Swift called out to her daughter, who was at that moment carrying in a bowl of chicken consommé that Martin had just prepared. Claire set down the bowl and hurried over.

"Mother," she said, sitting on the hard chair beside the bed. "Oh, what is it?"

Her mother turned her head and looked at her, eyes glazed. "Claire," she said in a thickened, altered voice, "are you going to go off with him again?"

Claire didn't know what to say; she and Martin hadn't been talking about the future. They had simply laid it aside for a while, concentrating on what was immediately in front of them. "I don't know," she answered.

"Well, would you make sure your father's okay before you leave?" said her mother. "Would you take care of him? I'm so worried that he'll completely fall apart on his own." Claire nodded. And then Maureen Swift's speech grew muted and peculiar and she talked of other subjects, one after another: a gingham dress she had worn when she was a child; the first date she'd had with Claire's father; a rainstorm that knocked down the family's fence in 1932, the year Claire was born. "There was water everywhere that night," her mother said, slow and soft, "just coming down for hours and hours. I thought it would never stop, and your father went out there in the pouring rain without a raincoat or boots or hat, and started to pick up the rails of the fence that were lying in the road. He wore a red plaid shirt, I remember."

And then Maureen Swift's voice died

away, growing fainter and fainter, as though she were walking down a long corridor. *Oh, Mother*, Claire thought to herself, starting to sob quietly as her mother turned her face to the wall and closed her eyes, *it's you who are leaving, not me.*

After Maureen Swift died, it was evident that Claire was still needed in her father's house. Lucas Swift was severely changed by his wife's death, and he had a great deal of trouble getting up in the morning and going over to his job at Swift Maintenance. Claire had to jump-start him each day, putting on the coffee for him, finding matching socks, making sure he knew exactly what equipment he needed to bring with him when he set off to work in the morning, seeing that he actually ate supper when he came home at night. Lucas Swift was in a fog of bereavement, and he didn't make much effort to leave it. Instead, he sat for long stretches on the tiny porch, rolling cigarettes for himself and staring off at the little square of land behind his house. He barely seemed to pay attention to anything that went on around him. Martin still hovered in the house during the day, helping Claire in any way he could, and Lucas didn't seem to mind his presence. Martin sometimes wondered whether Claire's father really knew he was there.

One night, when Claire was inside washing dishes and Martin was leaving the house to go back to the motel for the night, Lucas looked up at him from his spot on the porch and spoke.

"About my daughter," he said. "What are your plans?"

Martin was startled by this comment, mostly by the fact that Lucas was thinking in such a coherent way about Claire's life and her future. "My plans," Martin said gently, "are to marry her when we go back to London." Then he added, "Of course, we'd love it if you could come to the wedding. We'd find a way to bring you over."

Lucas Swift shook his head impatiently. "I won't be leaving this house, and I think you know that."

Yes, Martin did know that; Claire's father was not the type of person to suddenly break his routine, especially not now, after his wife's death.

"So what's the date that you'll be taking my girl away?" Lucas went on.

"Taking her away?" said Martin. "Mr.

Swift, I'm not *taking* her; I mean, she wants to go. She's twenty-one years old. And as far as when, well, I really can't say. Whenever Claire feels she's ready. When everything has been taken care of here."

"Oh," said Lucas Swift, "and when will that be? Will she let me know this time, or will she simply leave me a note and fly off in the night again?"

Martin looked downward. Claire's father was still angry with him because Martin had taken Claire from the fold, from a way of life that was never supposed to have been questioned. The only reason she was home again was because of something terrible. If it hadn't been for her mother's illness and death, she would still be off with Martin in a sun-filled flat in London above a small, fine restaurant, sculpting, making love, and living a kind of life that her father couldn't even begin to imagine. "I'm very sorry that I've made you and your family so unhappy," Martin said finally. "It certainly wasn't my intention."

After a while Lucas nodded; grudgingly he seemed to accept the apology. But Martin kept thinking about the question: when would Claire feel ready to go back to London with him? When would she feel as though everything here had been taken care of, and that she was free to go? There was always something more for her to do: a shirt of her father's with a hole at the elbow or knee that needed repair, an invoice to help him complete for a job Lucas had done downtown, an evening to sit with him in the living room after supper, just to make the approaching night bearable, just to make sure he wasn't too lonely and terrified to be an old man living without the woman he had married so long ago.

Neither Martin nor Claire addressed the question directly. Their home was in Kensington, near the gardens that Peter Pan had once visited in an old storybook, the little second-floor flat at 17 Dobson Mews. Both of them had felt very comfortable there, had liked the idea that this would be where they would stay, that this was where they had *landed*. But now the flat stood locked and empty; the sheets on the sleigh bed were cold. Neither of them knew when they might live there again.

Martin said good night to Claire's father and went back to the Lookout to sleep. In the morning, when he knew Lucas would be gone, he returned to the house and banged on the door, asking Claire if he could come in. He was agitated from the conversation of the night before and needed to speak to her right away. She was ironing her father's shirts one after the other, standing in the living room by the ironing board with the smell of soft, clean clothing scenting the air, and the hiss of the steam as the metal heel of the iron bore down on the fabric. "I'm afraid of what's happening," he said to her.

"What do you mean?" she asked, but of course she knew. Still her arm kept moving back and forth, methodically pressing her father's shirts.

"To you and me," he went on. "I feel stupid even mentioning any of this, but I can't help worrying a little. Our life in Europe—everything we did, everywhere we went, the foods we tried, and those train trips and how we felt, being together—it's all starting to feel like we made it up. What's that French expression—where two people have the same crazy thoughts? *Folie à deux*. But we didn't make it up, and it's not crazy." He paused, watching her carefully. "I guess what I'm saying is that I want to know we'll be together. I want to know that for sure."

Claire carefully set the iron upright and looked up. She and Martin faced each other across the narrow, unsteady surface of the ironing board.

"My father needs me now," Claire replied. "You've seen him, Martin; he's like someone who's been shipwrecked. He'd die without me."

"Then I'll stay here with you," said Martin.

"Here? What are you talking about?"

"I'll take a leave of absence from the restaurant and tell Duncan that I need to be in the States for a while," said Martin.

"But we still won't be able to live together here; we're not married, as I'm sure you remember."

Martin paused. He might have said to her in response, *Then we'll go down to New York City this minute and get married immediately, so grab your coat,* but he didn't. This was a grim time, not a time of celebration. They weren't settled, as they were supposed to have been. It wasn't the moment to marry, and both of them knew it.

"Well, I'll stay in town and we'll do what we can," was all he said. "We'll manage."

"But what will you do for work?" asked Claire. She herself was about to start helping out around Swift Maintenance, doing some of the lighter jobs, answering the phone and sending out invoices, a few of the tasks that her father had always executed effortlessly but that now seemed far beyond him.

"Well," said Martin, thinking quickly, "I'll go around to the different restaurants in the area and beg for work. I'll tell them I'm a desperate man."

"But you're not," she said.

He smiled. "I know," he said. "I just like the way it sounds." He paused. "Someone will hire me, Claire," he said. "I mean, I'm clean, I'm decent, I've got three years of a Princeton education. I can recite odes from my Introduction to Poetry class."

"Oh, well, *odes*," she said. "That will be a big help."

But she wasn't listening any longer. Instead, she walked around the front of the ironing board and swept him toward her, wrapping him in the angles of her delicate arms, gathering him in.

CHAPTER EIGHT

Over the next week, Martin borrowed a truck from Swift Maintenance and approached the managers of the four good restaurants in the area one by one: Glissando, a Northern Italian place located in Bright Valley, about twenty miles from Longwood Falls; the Publick House, about thirty miles north of town; the Columbine, a small, overpriced restaurant of indeterminate cuisine, located forty-two miles up Route 9; and even, in desperation, the glassed-in restaurant overlooking the eighth hole at Longwood Golf and Country, where Martin and his parents used to eat gluey chicken pot pies for Sunday dinner. But as it turned out, no one would hire him. For everyone, it seemed, had already received telephone calls from Ash Rayfiel, who had heard from local gossip that his son was back in town and was looking for work as a chef. Ash decided to make life difficult for Martin by either bribing the restaurant managers or threatening them. As far as he was concerned, a man simply can't drop out of Princeton, pocket a family heirloom and sell it (even if it's rightfully his), then run off to Europe to live illicitly with a woman from a lower social class, and expect that all will be forgiven when he returns home.

In fact, nothing was forgiven; although Martin had not laid eyes on his father since his return, the silent war continued between them. Finally, realizing that because of his father he was not going to get a good cooking job anywhere in the vicinity of Longwood Falls, in despair Martin went to the Longwood Diner, a sagging aluminum place with a sputtering neon sign, booths made of old, worn red leatherette patched up with electrical tape, and menus encased in smudged plastic. The crowd consisted of locals and truckers and teenagers out for a spin and a malt. For the most part the quality of food was poor; in the narrow, steaming kitchen, an indifferent short-order cook flipped frozen hamburger patties onto an irrevocably encrusted grill. Martin walked into the diner and asked to speak to the manager, reeling off his cooking experience and his desire for an immediate job. Miraculously, the manager, a heavy man with oiled hair who worked the cash register up front while listening to horse races on a radio, hired him on the spot. Ash Rayfiel had not thought to alert the manager of the diner that his son might come in and that he must not be hired. Apparently, it had never occurred to Ash that Martin would stoop so low for employment.

Martin and the manager shook hands on the deal, then Martin tied an apron around himself that was already soiled from God knows what. In the kitchen, the smell of meat and fried potatoes filled the air as Martin gratefully set to work.

Day in and day out he stood in his filthy apron at the grill in the primitive kitchen while waitresses shouted out a litany of orders. After work, Martin would drive back to the motel in the beat-up car he had bought cheaply, and quickly shower so that the smells were gone from him, and then he and Claire would meet. They would take long walks together, or sit and kiss in the maroon seats of the Longwood Cinema, or else they would simply go to his motel room and lie down together. Martin was exhausted all the time now; it wasn't just that he was working harder than he ever had before, it was also that the work was joyless. It was true that the diner staff turned out admirable malteds—the best Martin had ever tasted, rich and thick and flecked with vanilla bean—but their approach to cooking was rigid and uncreative. One day, when Martin tried to make the meat loaf taste better by adding a dollop of orange marmalade and some Dijon mustard to the ground meat, one of the waitresses, a sour woman with a head of blond hair as dry and stiff as a doll's, saw him do it and complained. "Our customers like their food plain and simple," she said. "So don't try that again."

He wasn't appreciated here, and he wasn't improving as a cook. His talents were on hold, he knew, and so were Claire's. Instead of sculpting and learning how to improve her skills, she was running the show at Swift Maintenance, then coming home to keep her lonely father company and clean the sad little house. By the time she and Martin were together in the evening, they were both equally tired and weary, and occasionally they snapped at each other. Once she bitterly criticized a shirt he wore, saying that its pattern was grotesquely ugly and made her dizzy just to look at it; another time he told her she was boring him to death when she talked at length about something that had happened at Swift Maintenance. They both apologized profusely after these unpleasant moments. Something had stolen over them, a dissatisfaction and a distinct sense that what was now happening to them had not been intended to happen. They ought to have been together, already married and on their own floating island in a city far from Longwood Falls, thinking of a long life together: love, babies, growing older, endless conversations before going to sleep. Flour and spices, red clay and water— these were supposed to be the ingredients of their life. What had happened? they both wondered with a sorrow and bewilderment they couldn't express.

"This is a very strange time," Martin whispered to her one evening as they lay in the motel bed beneath the blue coverlet. They had just made love, but Claire had seemed distant and distracted, her eyes as vague as smoke.

"Yes," she said. "It is."

"I wish," he said, "you could just come back with me to London. Can't your sister help out more? I mean, don't you think you've done enough? You don't have to be Saint Claire."

He was sorry as soon as he had said this. She looked at him coldly, now more distant than before. "I am not Saint Claire," she said. "You obviously don't have any idea of what it means to have an obligation to your family," she said. "To love them and want to help them. You have no idea of what it's like. And to answer your question: no, I haven't done enough. It's never enough. Don't you get it?" There was a pause; he didn't know what to say. "No," she went on, "I guess you don't."

They would always be different in this regard; she'd have an enormous sense of responsibility toward her family, and he'd have very little sense of responsibility toward his— or if he had such a sense, it had long been covered over by his anger. It wasn't until they had their own children, he thought, their own family, that they would find themselves on an even footing.

Actually, Martin admired her unwavering fidelity, a trait that colored her relationship with him as well. She was *his*; he knew that. She was a pretty girl who had caused men on the streets of Italy to look her over brazenly, as if assessing her: *Hmmm, very nice. Slender, long legs, the breasts just a bit too small, but the face is beautiful, and those eyes . . .* It didn't matter to them that she was always arm in arm with Martin; they had gazed at her with a frank and pleading expression, looking right past him. But she never took notice of them, not even the handsome, skinny-hipped ones who sat in the piazzas all day, as if they had nothing better to do, ice melting in their glasses.

She was his, but he couldn't have her fully, and she couldn't have him. He apologized to her now in bed at the Lookout Motel, telling her that he'd been insensitive. "Of course I know you can't come back to London with me just yet," he said. "I get frustrated, that's all. Please ignore it." Then he promised her that he would be more patient, and that eventually everything would return to the way it was supposed to be. Then they lay in silence in room 18, and he remembered the first time they had come here, and how, after making love, he had cooked her an omelette. They had eaten hungrily that day. It occurred to him now, having just made love with her again, that this time neither of them had an appetite.

As the weeks passed now, in moments of clarity it was impossible for Lucas Swift not to note how unhappy both his daughter and Martin had become. The Longwood Diner was no place for someone like Martin. If only he could find a job at a good restaurant, or perhaps could start a restaurant himself. But Martin had no money, a fact that Claire had mentioned to her father, but which Martin never brought up. It was as though he had passively accepted it and had no intention of fighting for it.

Late one Saturday afternoon in April, when Claire was out at a nearby farm overseeing Swift Maintenance's repairs to a barn, and Martin was at the diner dipping chicken pieces into boiling oil, Lucas Swift climbed into his truck that said SWIFT MAIN-

TENANCE on the side and drove down the street, heading toward a place he had always avoided as much as possible, a place of big houses, wide lawns, and small minds: the Crest.

The maid who answered the front door at the Rayfiel home took one look at Lucas Swift and said, "Service entrance is around back." She began to shut the door, but Lucas held out a hand to stop it.

"I'm not doing work here," he said. "I've come to see Mr. Rayfiel. Tell him it's Lucas Swift." He paused. "Claire's father," he pointedly added.

The maid looked doubtful, seeming not to believe that Ash Rayfiel would have anything to do with this scrawny old laborer who had the nerve to stand at the front door of the house as though he belonged here, but Lucas insisted, and so she silently retreated along the marble hallway.

A few moments later, the two men sat tensely in Ash Rayfiel's study. Many years earlier, long before Claire had ever met Martin, Lucas had been hired to build a garden wall for the Rayfiels, and when it came time for him to be paid, the Rayfiels' accountant insisted that the job was not up to par and that the payment would be half of what they had agreed upon. Lucas was astonished and outraged, for the wall was perfect, the bricks symmetrically laid and smoothly cemented along the boundary of the wide garden. He never knew for sure whether Martin's father himself was behind the incident, but he was fairly convinced he was. All the workers in town uniformly loathed Ash Rayfiel. Years later, when Claire announced she was in love with Ash's son, Lucas had felt an irrational anger and a burning memory of a bill for a garden wall that had remained only half paid.

But now, as he sat across the desk from Martin's father, he wasn't thinking about that wall or that bill. He was thinking only about Claire.

"What can I get you to drink?" Ash asked him.

Lucas shook his head. "Nothing, thank you," he said stiffly. Ash shrugged and reached for his pear-shaped decanter, pouring himself a tall drink of whiskey without water or ice, and taking a long swallow.

"Martin says you stole his money," Lucas began with difficulty.

Ash looked up over his glass, his eyebrows arching. "Oh, is that what he says?" he replied. "Well, it was my money to give, and it was mine to take back."

"He's having a hard time of it now," Lucas went on. "Ordinarily I wouldn't care. Ordinarily I'd say good, he deserves it. He's been living with my daughter in Europe—without the benefit of marriage—for half a year. But I believe he's decent, Mr. Rayfiel. Both of them are. They're young; they just want a little piece of happiness."

"Don't we all," said Ash.

"No one would hire him at any of the local restaurants," Lucas continued. "He felt that you were somehow behind it." Ash didn't comment, so Lucas went on. "If he could find some work that would challenge him, or else have his money back so that he could finance his own restaurant—"

"I had an unspoken deal with Martin," Ash interrupted Lucas. "I provided that certain money would be waiting for him when he reached twenty-one not because he was my son, but because he would be running my business. Hats. I didn't give it to him so he would have a head start in life, but so that he would be up to speed." He paused. "But Martin chose not to go into hats. He thinks hats are a ridiculous thing to spend your life on. He thinks I'm a ridiculous, spiteful man, I guess." Ash Rayfiel drew in a hard breath. "No, I didn't steal his money. I simply withdrew it."

"And if the money makes the difference between misery and happiness?" asked Lucas.

Ash Rayfiel played with his glass. He moved it to the left, then to the right. Finally he replaced it precisely on its original ring of sweat, and said, "You do understand *he* stole from *me*."

Lucas Swift didn't answer.

"He took the family crest," Ash said. "An object that had been in my family for a century. Fortunately, just this month I received a report from an alert jeweler in Amsterdam who's had some experience with objects that have wandered from their rightful owner. He did the research into who the rightful owner of this particular object might be, and he and I came to mutually acceptable terms. The money doesn't matter to me, and the sentiment doesn't matter to me either. But the dishonesty does."

"He says it was his," cut in Lucas.

"Oh, yes, in a generous moment his

grandfather gave it to him at birth," said Ash, "but again that was with an understanding that he keep it. That he display it. That he act like a goddamn proud member of the Rayfiel family." Ash finished his drink and smiled thinly. "I don't enjoy this, you know," he said. "I wish my son were different. I miss the adoring little boy in gray flannel knickers and a cap who used to follow me around the factory and ask about the 'bims.'" He glanced up at Lucas. *"Brims."* He smiled to himself, and then the smile turned into something hard and immovable. "I wish my son were different," he said again. "I wish my wife didn't drink before lunch. I wish the hat business were more interesting. But you play the cards you're dealt, and if you don't like the rules, then you get out of the game and you don't look back. But that's not what Martin's done, and there's nothing I can do about that or about who he is or who I am— or, for that matter, about how interesting or uninteresting hats are."

Ash Rayfiel's glass of whiskey had been like a kind of hourglass; now that the drink was finished, the meeting was over. Ash stood. Lucas stood. The two men didn't shake hands. Ash simply opened the door,

and Lucas walked out, and as he walked
through the long hall, he felt sorry for Martin
for having grown up here amid such splen-
dor and indifference.

That night, when Claire was folding her
clothing in the bedroom of her father's
house and getting ready for sleep, Lucas
Swift came and stood in the doorway.
"Claire," he said, "I need to speak with you."
   "Sure," she said. "Is everything okay?"
   "You and Martin," he said. "I want you to
go back to London together. As soon as you
can arrange it."
   Claire was startled; she stared at him.
"What do you mean?" she asked. "Why do
you want us to leave?"
   "It won't work out for you here," he said.
   "How do you know that?" she asked.
   "I spoke to his father," he began.
   Claire's mouth dropped open. "You *spoke*
to him?" she cried. "But Martin will be furi-
ous."
   "I wanted to see if that man would ever
give in," said Lucas. "And he won't. He's in
a rage at his son, and it's just going to burn
and burn, Claire. So I want you to go."
   "But what about you?"

"Oh, I'll be all right," said her father.

"I worry about you," she said. "How you'll manage."

"There's nothing to worry about," he said, but his voice was flat.

That night, in his sleep, Lucas Swift thought he heard his wife, Maureen, call out to him. For one confused moment he believed she was alive, and that she was still sleeping in Claire's room. He bolted from bed in the darkness and out into the hallway, where he tripped over a small table and fell to the floor in a heap, badly spraining his ankle. Claire, hearing the crash, came hurrying out to him.

"Oh, Dad," she said, snapping on a light and crouching down beside him. And as she looked at him in the light of her bedroom she saw how frail he appeared, his shoulders in his thin blue shirt narrow, his back stooped. His ankle was already swelling. He was on a path of decline, and it would accelerate greatly if she left him now. Her father knew it, too; they both did. She helped him up and when he put weight on his ankle, the pain made him inhale sharply, surprised. What he had said to her before bed was that she should leave and live her own life with Martin because this was their moment. She should leave immediately and thrive, but when she left her father would sink quickly. Here was only one small example of what was in store for him.

Would you take care of him? her mother had asked, and she had nodded yes. It was the decent thing to do. She wouldn't leave her father, not like this. She couldn't leave Martin, either, but in some way she would have to, at least for a while. To be more exact about it, he would have to leave *her.* He would have to go back to 17 Dobson Mews, where he had begun to make his name. She knew that he would achieve many things, that he would continue doing the kind of cooking he had always loved, in a kitchen equipped with pots and ladles in a hundred different sizes and an acreage of counter space where he could spread out to work and various small, strange tools—such as the mandoline he'd once showed her, not trying to hide his delight in an instrument that could instantly shred a potato into a few dozen perfect, translucent coins. He was very much at home in the restaurant in London, living in the little flat and exploring the greengrocers and the exotic spice stores and haggling prices with the fishmongers. He would do his work seriously and become successful in London; she had no doubt about it.

For now, Claire would stay here and be with her father, as her mother had wanted. She and Martin would be together again as soon as they could, although neither of them had any idea of when. As she helped her father back to bed and brought him some ice for his ankle, he glanced at her. Then he sighed lightly, sadly, because he must have known from her expression that she had made her decision, and that she wasn't going anywhere.

Throughout the spring, Claire and Martin debated the subject of whether Martin should go back to London without her. At first he absolutely refused to go, saying that his life was here with her, but after a while he began to relent, seeing that the life they had here was in fact doing neither of them any good. With great reluctance, he bought a one-way ticket to London on a flight leaving New York City early on the morning of May 28.

The night before his voyage was the

fourth anniversary of their first encounter in the gazebo, and it was important to both of them to be together there, as they had done every year on this date. So at dusk they sat under the white roof, both of them full of dread at the thought of his departure in the morning. It was starting to rain slightly, the town square looking like a pastel drawing that has gotten smudged. A few people hurried off in different directions, fumbling to open umbrellas.

"I bought you something," she said to him. "A going-away gift." And then she handed him a large white box.

"You didn't need to get me anything," Martin said, but he was clearly pleased, and when he opened it he saw the briefcase inside, a caramel color, with his initials discreetly stamped in gold on the side. "Claire," he said, astonished, "where did you get this? I saw one just like it when we were in Florence, remember? We had spent hours at the Uffizi, you never wanted to leave, and on the way to the hotel we—"

"I know," she said. "I wrote to the shop—Cuoio di Lipari, I remembered it was called—and I asked them to send it to me."

"But how could you afford it?"

"I've been saving up," she said softly. "I wanted you to have something nice to carry all your recipes and papers and everything in."

"It makes me look like a businessman," he said, lifting the beautiful case up by its thick handle. "The son my father always wanted," he added with some irony, then he put the case down. "I love it," he said. "I'll carry it for a long, long time. Until I'm old."

She smiled slightly, embarrassed and pleased. "I can't imagine you old," she said.

"You will," he said.

The rain had grown heavier now, the clouds suddenly gathering, the sky turning unnaturally dark. Somewhere off in the direction of the hills came thunder, a warning sound. Claire moved closer to Martin on the wooden seat of the gazebo.

"Promise me," she suddenly said, "that you'll come to meet me at the gazebo every year on May twenty-seventh at dusk. No matter what." He didn't say anything. "Promise me," she said again, more urgent this time.

"I promise," he said. "And you promise me that you'll be there."

"I promise," she said.

He lifted her hair from the nape of her neck, and whispered something to her that she couldn't quite hear. Slowly he opened her blouse, slipping the tiny buttons, no bigger than raindrops, through their eyelets one by one. No one was watching; the rain had made everyone scatter and now they were alone. "You're so beautiful," he said, coming forward and putting his face into the shadow between her breasts.

Then they sank down together onto the cool floor of the gazebo. She pulled him against her, thinking: *How can he be leaving? How has this happened to us?*

Lightning intermittently shot across the sky, illuminating parts of their bodies: now a mouth, a hand, a breast, a shoulder. Neither of them could speak or be heard. They were both silently crying, their faces wet in the stuttering white lightning that divided the sky high above their gazebo.

CHAPTER NINE

They kept their promise. Every year on May 27 they met at the gazebo at dusk. The first year after he had moved back to London he arrived at the gazebo before her and was sitting very still when she came running across the diagonal path toward him in a yellow dress splashed with a floral pattern, her face flushed. The second year, two little boys were sitting in the gazebo when they arrived, legs swinging, studiously examining a stack of baseball cards, actually having the nerve to continue to sit there even though this was Martin and Claire's place. And the third year after they had made the promise to each other, Claire was waiting for Martin on May 27.

His plane had been late, and so the sky was fading into a stone gray by the time he arrived in Longwood Falls, tired from the trip. In a way, he was tired from the entire year he'd spent without her. They wrote each other often, and spoke on the phone when they could, but the time difference made telephone calls difficult to choreo-graph, and Martin's work hours were unpre-dictable. There were many times at the restaurant when something would happen— some small triumph or slight—and all he wished was that she was there to talk to in bed at night. It was a simple wish: to be with the woman he loved, both of them quiet and sleepy and settling in for the night. To talk and talk as late as they wanted. To wake up in the morning and there she would be, that half smile on her face even in her sleep. But he couldn't have what he wanted, and the deprivation was wearing him down in small, almost imperceptible ways. When he arrived at the gazebo, they always sank against each other in relief, and it was minutes be-fore either of them pulled back.

When Martin agreed to move back to London for a while and leave Claire here to tend to her father and her father's business, he had never planned on being gone permanently. They assumed they would be together for good one of these days, and yet one chaotic year had turned into another. They now led two separate lives but were still connected in some basic, irrevocable way, writing and calling and meeting at the gazebo on each anniversary. It wasn't just Martin who was worn down by the absences, the back and forth, the dissatisfaction; Claire seemed somewhat unhappy lately, too, and slightly remote, as though she had some hidden sadness that she couldn't yet talk about. He didn't press it.

He had begun to realize, as the years unfolded, that Claire was slowly transforming from the girl he had met here eight years earlier. Now her pale hair had a shadow of darker russet in it, and there was a tiredness to her eyes. She worked so hard helping her father and barely had time to think, or take a walk, or do anything just for herself. "Do you get a chance to sculpt?" he asked her today at the gazebo.

She nodded and said, "Sometimes." She was evasive now, he realized, and it troubled him. Evasiveness was a new quality for Claire, who had always been so open and expressive. But he himself had new qualities, too, he knew, which had come from living in a foreign culture and being steeped in it for such a long time.

And now 17 Dobson Mews was his. Duncan Lear had defected to the town of Exeter in southwest England, where his new restaurant, Duncan's Grill, was booming. In his absence, and perhaps in the absence of the feeling of being *watched* by Duncan, Martin had achieved a rapid success as a chef, and had been written about in the London papers as the new force behind the wonderful restaurant in Kensington. Eventually Martin was asked by a team of investors if he would like to join their group in a bid to buy the restaurant. Martin's financial contribution could be merely a token, but he would have to agree to stay on and run the kitchen.

"You can rename the place whatever you like," offered one of the investors. "Perhaps Martin's. Or Rayfiel's."

He shook his head; he didn't want his own name up on a sign. Perhaps he would call the place Claire's, and when she was able to live here with him again everyone would know her as the lovely, slender American who had a top restaurant in her name. But Claire was a modest person, and would be embarrassed having a restaurant named after her. Suddenly, the right name occurred to him: the Gazebo.

When the new owners took over, the architects constructed a soaring octagonal ceiling inside the main dining room. They also, at Martin's instruction, made the large plate-glass windows even bigger, giving the restaurant the airy, wraparound feeling of its namesake. Within days of its opening, the newly christened restaurant was mentioned in the London *Times,* which called dining there "bliss." Sometimes, when Martin stepped out of the gleaming white-tiled kitchen, patrons would wave to him, and he would go over and say hello. Women often flirted with Martin; there was one woman in particular who often came to dinner, a beautiful but serious Englishwoman named Frances Banks with a heavy brown braid down her back and a rotating collection of fine linen clothes. She had already been married to a much older Cambridge don and had been widowed, leaving her to raise their young daughter, Louisa, whom she occasionally brought to the resturant with her. Frances Banks was made up of compelling angles, and she was both well bred and irreverent. Distantly, Martin realized he liked Frances's ironic wit and her good looks, and he took note of the way she gazed at him.

One day she had said, "I was just thinking how lucky your wife is to have you cook like this for her all the time."

"I don't have a wife," he found himself replying, and he immediately regretted it, realizing that the point of her question had been to find out his marital status. In his heart he did feel married to Claire, even though he had not seen her since last May 27, when they had spent an hour at the gazebo before parting. He had asked Claire to come to the Lookout Motel with him that day, where he was staying, but she had declined, saying that she had to get home. But he knew it was almost too dangerous to go back in that direction, to lie together in that bed. If they did, they would find their separation unbearable. As it was, his visits were always brief; even so, they were almost too much, too painful a reminder of what they didn't have the rest of the year. Nonetheless, Martin was committed to Claire for life;

their letters back and forth across the Atlantic were slightly less frequent lately but were still both ardent and tender. He wished he had said to Frances, "Yes, my wife loves my cooking. The first time we made love I cooked her an omelette."

He hurried back to the kitchen after this conversation, and when Frances and her daughter returned to the Gazebo two days later, Martin did not poke his head into the dining room to say hello. A waiter came in and said that Mrs. Banks was asking for the pleasure of Mr. Rayfiel's company, if only for a moment, but Martin sent the waiter out to apologize to Mrs. Banks and say that he was too busy today to leave his post.

Now Martin sat with Claire in the gazebo, leaning against her and gently holding her. She was still his, though her father had recently developed arthritis in both knees and had trouble with mobility. The fact was, her father now needed her more than ever, and the tone of the letters had begun to shift accordingly. Instead of mentioning with certainty that they would be together soon, Martin and Claire simply neglected to broach the issue. All they knew for sure was that they still loved each other as fully as ever, and that they would see each other every May 27 at the gazebo, "come hell or high water," Martin had written to her.

In the evenings in Longwood Falls, he knew, father and daughter sat on the back porch and talked as the sun set. Lucas Swift often told Claire that she should hightail it to London where she belonged, but when she replied that she was needed here, with him, he did not argue. In addition to the way she took complete care of her father, she also had come to oversee the family business. Swift Maintenance was doing very well, thanks to Claire's attentions. She had proven to be a precise bookkeeper and had a real skill at dealing with customers and workers. She could not get away yet; neither could Martin. Both of them knew it, and there was an unspoken disappointment that inflected this year's meeting at the gazebo.

But there was something else in the air today, too. Claire didn't merely look older than she used to, or more tired; she also looked apprehensive. As it turned out, there was a reason.

"Listen to me," she said to Martin, and she took both his hands in hers. "I have to tell you something."

His first thought was that one of his parents had died. He felt his back stiffen at the idea; although he had not spoken to his mother or father in years, he prepared himself for the news. But what Claire said instead was, "I've met someone."

Her voice was miserable, full of regret.

Martin paused. "What do you mean?" he asked, although he was afraid he knew what she meant.

"His name is Daniel Clusker," she said quietly.

Martin barely knew how to respond. How could she have met someone? They had an agreement, a pact. They were going to be together someday.

"How *could* you?" Martin finally asked, and he stood unsteadily, then slammed his fist against one of the wooden supports of the gazebo.

"Stop!" she said, going over to him, watching him shake out his hand in pain. "Please," she went on, frantically now, "I didn't know what to do. I'm here, and you're there, and you seem so unhappy all the time, Martin, so totally worn out by our being in separate places. And I've tried to find a way to make it work; it's all I've thought about. But the years keep going by and we never confront it anymore—what's going to happen to us. Where this is all going to end up. You know I love you. You know you're my entire life. But Daniel came and helped out, and he's very good with my father, and he's reliable. And I know how lonely you are; I can see it every year. More than lonely. You're disappointed. It's taken something out of you. So I decided to be the first one to do something," she said. She took a breath, and in a quiet voice she added, "And now you're free to do the same."

He stared at her, feeling the blood beating inside him, feeling his injured hand throb with its own separate beat. "Just tell me one thing," he said, his voice thick and unfamiliar to himself. "This Daniel Clusker..." He spoke the name coldly. "Do you actually love him?"

Claire looked down at her lap. "He's a very kind person," she said simply, and her reply reminded Martin of Nicole's answer to the question about her husband, Thierry. *He is a good father,* Nicole had said, as if that were enough. Was it enough? Who decided what was enough for one person, what was satisfactory, what made a decent life? "Daniel can fix anything," Claire was saying. "He does handsprings. He knows the name of every bird. He's very thoughtful." Then she looked up, took another breath, and said, "He asked me to marry him."

Martin stared. *"And?"* he said.

"And I told him I would," she said quietly. "I couldn't think what else to say."

Martin felt a sourness burst in the back of his throat. "Claire, come to London with me tonight," he said.

"You know I can't," she said. "My father. The business—"

"Then I'll move here," he tried. "I'll give up the whole stupid restaurant."

"It's not stupid," she said. "It's what you've always wanted."

"Yes," he said. "It is." He thought about the softly lit room of the restaurant, and the way it felt to stand and observe from the kitchen door as the first customers of the evening were shown to their tables. The things he felt were contentment, accomplishment, calm. But then he thought about the fact that he would never make love to Claire again, would never marry her or have children with her. Maybe once a year they would still briefly meet each other, as they had sworn they always would, but that was all.

"You're really going to do this?" he asked.

She looked away and nodded.

"So that's it, then?"

She nodded again.

"I have to go now, Claire," Martin said. He picked up the briefcase she had given him and walked down the white steps, staggering slightly, like a man who has drunk too much champagne, or has been given some sudden and very bad news.

Daniel Clusker was a carpenter Claire had hired to work for Swift Maintenance, a man who lived in the next town. He was tall and red-haired, and she liked him right away when he came into the front office of the maintenance company. He was charming in a soft-spoken, offhand way, and they talked for a little longer than might have been expected.

Later, when Claire was walking through the town square, she saw some of the workmen sitting and having lunch. Daniel Clusker was among them, and he was amusing the other men by turning an impressive series of handsprings on the grass. When he noticed Claire, he quickly got to his feet, embarrassed, and gave a small wave. Daniel was charming but deeply, bewilderingly shy. So Claire was surprised when, the following day, he came by again and asked her if she was free that night.

"Free?" she asked, not comprehending.

"You know. Available," he said. "I thought we could go somewhere. I promise I won't talk about carpentry."

So, for some reason she didn't even understand, she went with him, and he was true to his word, not discussing carpentry at all. They drove through the hills in his pickup truck, and Daniel pointed out particular trees, and trails he had hiked with his brothers. He was an amateur naturalist, someone who particularly loved birds. He owned four pairs of binoculars of different strengths.

They had supper together at his house—nothing elaborate, just some soup and a salad—and he played a few old Louis Armstrong records he liked. Sometimes during the day he would come say hello, wearing his work shirt and tool belt. Claire couldn't decide whether or not he was actually flirting with her. She hadn't paid any attention to men other than Martin for so long. Why in the world was she paying attention to this one?

At first she told herself that her reaction was only one of kindness. Daniel Clusker was sweet, and he was lonely. But it occurred to her that maybe, even though Martin would never admit it, he secretly wanted her to meet someone else, and that she was responding to his unspoken wish. Maybe he wanted her to make a break now, just at the point that his restaurant in London was turning into a big success. That way, he could feel the loss of Claire and mourn her and then move on, perhaps finding someone himself. She knew how much he hated going to sleep alone in the sleigh bed in the flat above the restaurant, where they were supposed to have lived together. Once, lying in that bed with Claire, Martin had tried to describe for her the loneliness of having been an only child, and how different this was, being with somebody, and she thought of that lonely child now, and how he was becoming a lonely man.

Was this what Martin secretly wanted, perhaps without even knowing it? Or was this what she needed to tell herself, what she wanted to believe, in order to allow herself to let Martin go? Even if he didn't want it, it had begun to occur to her that maybe she ought to give it to him anyway—that maybe she ought to force the issue. Martin would never leave her on his own; he would have to be pushed out into the world. Martin was at his best with a woman beside him, someone to tell everything to, someone to touch him; he'd said as much, over and over. He needed comfort, and while she wanted to be the one to give it to him, she couldn't, at least not often enough, and she didn't know when she'd be able to.

And comfort—this was something that Claire needed, too. And then she'd thought of Daniel Clusker—his fair eyelashes, his shyness, his attentiveness. Would he do? Maybe he would.

That was two months earlier; a great deal had happened since then. Claire had let Daniel bring her a bunch of freesia and a box of saltwater taffy and even—ironically— a funny Tyrolean hat that he'd picked up at a local fair and thought she'd like. He didn't know that she never wore hats; she realized that he didn't know much about her at all.

One afternoon Daniel had picked Claire up at work and driven her home in his pickup, and neither of them talked to each other the entire way, as though they knew something was up but couldn't acknowledge it directly. When he stopped the truck in front of her house, he'd turned off the ignition, composed himself for a moment, then leaned across the seat and kissed her.

Claire closed her eyes when he did this, not only because that was what you were supposed to do during a kiss, but because she couldn't bear to watch this thing she had set in motion.

July 3, 1956

Dear Martin,
I'm writing to let you know that Claire is getting married here at the old stone church on Glimmer Road on July 17 at eleven in the morning. I know how awful this must be for you, but still I thought you'd want to know the date. Sorry, Martin; I really am.

As ever,
Hush

Although she never knew it, Martin came back to town and stood across the road from the small country church where Claire and

Daniel had just been married. He watched as the new husband and wife came out of the church doors, and saw the way their friends and family tossed a small hailstorm of rice at them. Daniel Clusker was a red-haired man with fair, freckly skin. He threw an arm around his new bride and kissed her on the mouth while Martin looked on, dazed. Claire's pale face was flushed, her hair decorated with lilies, her dress long and white and simple. Her little niece and nephew—Margaret's twins—played on the stone steps of the old church, picking up grains of rice and throwing them at each other. And there was Claire's father, dressed in a morning coat and being helped out of the building by two young, strong men. Lucas Swift had deteriorated greatly, Martin saw, watching as Claire's father took a couple of careful, stiff steps with his arthritic knees.

Daniel Clusker and his wife climbed into a car that was waiting in front of the church. *Claire Clusker,* Martin thought bitterly as he stood behind a sycamore. What a clumsy, wrongheaded name. He was hidden from view behind some thick bunches of leaves, and he watched the bride and groom drive off together, a string of tin cans clanking noisily from the bumper of their car.

The next night, Martin returned to London. He slept hard on the airplane, his head against the window, not hearing the stewardess when she came by offering a choice of dinners from a cart. And when the plane landed he went straight to the restaurant, not even bothering to stop upstairs to shave or wash up or check his mail. Cooking would help him, he thought; it would send everything else away from his mind, and the only thing that would remain would be whether the sauce he was stirring needed more salt.

Later, during the hectic evening, a waiter came in and said that Mrs. Banks was dining with her daughter tonight and wondered if Mr. Rayfiel might come out and say hello.

"I'm sorry," Martin started to say to the waiter, as he had done before. "Please tell her—" Then he paused, remembering the way Claire had looked at her wedding, her cheeks a high color, her hair floating up around her face. "Tell her," he went on, "that I'll be right there." And he put down his ladle, wiped his hands on a dish towel, and walked out through the swinging doors.

Frances Banks was sitting with her six-year-old daughter at a corner table, sharing a dessert plate of wild berries strewn over homemade ginger ice cream. She put down her spoon as Martin approached and said to her daughter, "Look, darling, here's the chef." She paused, then smiled a slow, wry smile, adding, "And he's in desperate need of a shave."

Within a week, Martin was invited to her house in Bloomsbury. It was a sprawling place, scattered with books that had belonged to her late husband, as well as many pieces of doll clothing and doll furniture that belonged to Louisa. In the corner, Martin noticed a small bronze sculpture of a mother and child. Claire would love that piece, he thought to himself. Frances noticed him staring at it and asked him what he was thinking. "Nothing," he told her. Then he turned to her, and in a calm, easy voice, he said, "Let's go to bed."

Frances was a woman who had been married and borne a child; she was a seasoned person, worldly and sexually complex. He lay with her in her huge featherbed and thought of the sleigh bed where he and Claire had made love. *Stop,* he told himself.

Stop thinking about Claire. For surely Claire, who according to Hush was on her honeymoon at a hotel in the Pennsylvania Dutch country right now, was not thinking about Martin as she lay in bed with Daniel Clusker. Or was she?

The thought occurred to him as he kissed and caressed the unfamiliar, warm body of Frances Banks. She had fuller hips and breasts than Claire. Everything about her was weightier, more voluptuous, and yet Claire was the one who resonated. Claire rang out, even as Martin made love to this new woman in her Bloomsbury home. "Claire!" he said in a light, choked cry during lovemaking that first night with Frances. She heard him, and he was embarrassed.

"It's all right," she assured him later as they lay together drinking the wine that she earlier had put in a brass bucket of melting ice beside the bed. "I know about her." She lit a cigarette with a lighter that had her late husband's initials on it.

He raised his eyebrows. "Oh?" he said.

"I asked around," said Frances. "Tried to find out why you were avoiding me. And the maître d' gave me my answer."

"How did he know?" asked Martin.

"Oh," said Frances, "he said many people know. Your friend Duncan Lear may be a great person, but apparently he's not very discreet."

Martin propped himself up on an elbow and regarded her. "So what do you think about all of this?" he asked.

She shrugged and brushed her hair from her face. "I think," she began, "that I'm a woman who is too young to be a widow forever. I'm only thirty years old."

"I'm twenty-four," said Martin.

"It doesn't matter," said Frances. "We don't have to be exactly the same."

Mrs. Frances Banks was telling him she wasn't exactly like him, nor he like her, and that she didn't care, but she was telling him more than this, too. She was saying that she wanted to make an arrangement with him. He could call out the name of another woman in bed, and she wouldn't care. She was attracted to him and taken by him, and wished him to be with her, to make her less lonely, and to give her young daughter a father.

It would be an arrangement, but probably that was what Claire had with Daniel Clusker. He kept her company, made her life in

Longwood Falls more bearable. Martin hoped Claire was happy, hoped Daniel was wonderful to her. And he hoped that she was still sculpting, that she never stopped.

So much had been given up, Martin thought as he lay stunned in this new bed: the wedding he and Claire would never have, the children they would never have, with her pale hair and his dark eyes. "Our children will be artistically talented," Claire had once said, a long time ago, "as well as great cooks."

"I pity them," Martin had responded. "Artistic cooks. They won't have it easy in life."

"No," Claire had said. "They won't. But when we're old, they'll cook bland, digestible food for us, and arrange it on the plate in very creative designs."

Now he could almost see these phantom children he'd never meet or swing into the air or take to the first day of school or carry on his shoulders above a crowd. Frances's daughter, Louisa, was a lovely, shy girl of six with her mother's thick braid of auburn hair, and something tragic around the eyes and mouth, the result of having lost her father to a coronary when she was just two years old. Martin liked Louisa and knew that if he stayed in Frances's life he would in fact become a father to this little girl. It didn't seem such a bad idea. He couldn't promise Frances the sun, moon and stars, but she wasn't asking for them either. Apparently, the great love of her own life had been her late husband James, a philosophy scholar she had studied with at Cambridge, and whom she had worshipped until his death.

Now she didn't want passionate love from Martin. It was true that she wanted passion, and it was also true that she wanted something resembling love, but the two, he had come to realize, didn't need to be offered in one heaping serving. She would take what she could get, and so would he. They had an understanding.

When Martin Joseph Rayfiel married Frances Antonia Banks at a small ceremony at a well-maintained Anglican church in London on August 18, 1956—a month after Claire's wedding—he did not send a wedding announcement to the love of his life on the other side of the ocean. It would have been cruel. He was still angry with Claire for starting this chain of events, but he didn't blame her anymore. It all made a strange kind of sense now. On Martin and Frances's honeymoon in Positano, they stayed in a beautiful house on the water with stands of lemon trees nearby. The fruit reminded him of the way Claire smelled. He was being haunted by her scent on his own honeymoon, as though she were a ghost that was lingering in the tiled rooms of the house. But Claire wasn't a ghost; she was a living, breathing woman, someone he could not have. Martin drank heavily on his honeymoon and often sat outside smoking, a habit he usually disliked. Frances had to call him inside. "It's dark," she said, coming up behind him and draping her arms loosely around his neck. "Why don't you come in for the night?"

Reluctantly Martin stood, tamping out his cigarette and breathing in the citrus smell of the trees all around him—a smell he knew and loved so deeply—and then he turned and went inside the house with the woman who was his wife.

CHAPTER TEN

It was the middle of the night by the time Abby learned of Claire's and Martin's marriages to other people. When she heard the news on one of the tapes, she had to stand and pace around the silent hallways of the *Ledger*. She walked back and forth, unable to be still. In all the offices, the lights were off and the computers were either bright and dotted with the dancing pattern of a screen saver, or totally dark. Everyone who worked at the newspaper was off in their different homes, most of them now fast asleep beside a husband, wife, or lover. Abby thought about packing up for the night and returning to her own home, but she couldn't stop now. She was curious, of course; she knew now that she could no longer look into the eyes of those photographs from fifty years earlier and say how the story was going to end. But more than curiosity was impelling Abby now. It was also her anger with Claire.

Claire could have gone back. She *should* have gone back. Abby herself had returned to Longwood Falls because she wanted to preserve the *Ledger* and her father's work—but also because she had nothing to keep her in New York City. Nothing she'd allowed to keep her in New York City, anyway; an occasional phone call from a shaggy-haired young pediatrician didn't count. Claire, however, had Martin. She had a life waiting for her in London. Abby couldn't understand the logic of Claire's decision to take care of her father, or of Claire's decision to get married to Daniel Clusker, and Martin's copycat decision to marry Frances Banks. And that was just it; these were decisions based on logic, lives led according to the demands of reason, whereas Claire and Martin's relationship was based on love. Love versus logic—it all came down to that. Abby felt almost protective of what Claire and Martin had had, wishing that she'd been there all those many years ago to counsel them, to tell them *don't do it* when they were about to get married to this other man and woman.

Abby returned to her own office now and peered inside the briefcase again. She found a tin ring with a small green stone set in it; it was the ring from Claire's *mystère* dessert at a café in the south of France, so long ago. Then she found a wedding announcement from the *Longwood Falls Ledger*—the very paper she now ran—yellow and flaking and over forty years old, held together between two sheets of plastic, announcing the marriage of Claire Swift to Daniel Clusker. She found another wedding announcement—this one much grander, and with a photograph above it—from the society pages of a London paper the following month, showing Martin posing beside a formidably attractive woman. Both of them appeared somber and contemplative. Abby also found clippings from several London newspapers and magazines about Martin's restaurant, the Gazebo. There was a picture of him in his tall white chef's toque, standing and holding a roast game hen on a silver plate. There was an old, cracking lunch menu from the restaurant, too, dated March 8, 1958, and which read as follows:

APPETIZERS

Chilled melon soup garnished with crystallised ginger

Shrimp salad with leeks, tomato, and coriander

Endive, watercress, and mushroom salad, with an orange mustard vinaigrette

MAIN COURSES

Chicken "Claire." Breast of chicken dredged with pecans and served on a bed of rice with currants

Classic macaroni and cheese. American style, with a broiled, bread-crumb crust

Porterhouse steak. Served with a green peppercorn sauce and potato-parsnip puree

Broiled mahogany lobster. Out of the shell, glazed with a Japanese-style soy-honey finish, and served with fragrant rice

DESSERTS

New York cheesecake, with a graham-cracker crust and fresh berries

Peach cobbler, served warm with homemade
ginger ice cream

Plate of Martin's assorted warm cookies

Devil's food cake. Three layers, with
bittersweet frosting,
on a pool of crème anglaise

This meal had been cooked and served
more than forty years ago, but still Abby felt
as though she could imagine the individual
flavors and could see Martin at the stove,
whisking a pat of butter into a pot of something, letting it swirl and dissolve. But when
she imagined him in his home life, married
to Frances Banks and living in London with
her and her daughter, Abby pictured an un-
smiling man, his face grown slightly gaunt
and tired because of the resignation that
guided his life.

Abby carefully put the old menu aside,
and beneath it she found a birth announcement, dated April 3, 1958, and printed on
stiff paper with a delicate pink border. "Mr.
and Mrs. Daniel Clusker are pleased to announce the birth of a daughter, Alison Martina Clusker, 7 lbs., 2 oz." The baby's middle

name caused Abby to take in a sharp breath.

Slowly she sat back down in her chair. Maybe there was more to Claire than Abby had imagined; maybe there was more to this woman who would honor her private past in such a candid way. Abby turned the cassette player back on. The middle of the night had come and gone, but now Abby knew she would not sleep at all before the morning.

Alison Martina Clusker. The first and middle names were, on the surface, appealing and benign, a collection of pretty syllables fitting this baby who had her mother's pale skin and eyes and delicate features, but her father Daniel's shock of bright red hair. But beneath the surface of those syllables lay Claire's tribute to Martin. Claire had spoken frankly to Daniel about Martin before she agreed to marry him, telling him that she and Martin had been lovers and now they were not, but that they still cared about each other very deeply and would always meet at the gazebo once a year on their anniversary. Daniel hadn't liked the idea of it, but he had simply nodded and thanked her for telling him, and then he hadn't wanted to talk about it anymore. Of course Daniel knew how she had arrived at the baby's middle name. Half the town of Longwood Falls knew, too, but if they gossiped about it—which they surely did—then Claire never found out. No one dared to spread any false stories, such as a suggestion that Martin—not Daniel—was really the baby's father. Just one look at that baby's fiery red hair told them that was ridiculous. Alison was Daniel's child through and through, but the stories about Claire's love affair with Martin were still told in Longwood Falls, a kind of local folkloric legend: the rich boy and the poor girl, and how they had lived abroad in sin and tried for a life together and ultimately, like all sinners, failed.

Claire would never be unfaithful to Daniel with Martin; there was no question of that. And yet her deeper sense of faithfulness *was* to Martin. He was the man who knew her. They would always know each other in this way; not even marriage could touch that.

During the wedding ceremony, Claire and Daniel had promised each other fidelity. Although she never felt particularly moved by their lovemaking, she felt a kind of reassurance when she was in bed with him. He came home at the end of a long day of carpentry, his body smelling of cedar shavings—a kind of delicious, almost edible scent, she thought—and Claire returned from work, too, and sometimes they lay down in the high bed in their house on Conley Lane, and he eased himself on top of her, as though afraid he might hurt her with his hard, workman's body. His skin was freckled, a fact that was slightly displeasing to her the first time she saw it, but which she grew used to. He was a seriously sweet man, someone who could speak of table saws and circular saws for hours if Claire would let him—which she wouldn't. He made love like one of his saws: easing back and forth with an almost mechanical rhythm. She didn't mind it—in fact, sometimes it was quite nice—but it bore so little resemblance to her overwhelming experience of making love with Martin, that the two couldn't be placed in the same category. Still, lying in bed with Daniel kept the long winter nights less lonely; they would often talk quietly about what they had done that day, or about her father, whom Daniel was very close to, or about the baby, who they often brought into the bed in the middle of the night to be nursed.

Claire loved nursing Alison, loved feeling the grate and tug on her nipple and watching the baby extract the milk with impressive greed. Two years after redheaded Alison, Claire gave birth to a son, Jonathan, and then fourteen months after him came a surprise baby, another son named Edward. Now Claire was surrounded; this was what she had wanted, wasn't it? To have all these people all around her, the cacophony of being in a family. The children still needed milk as they grew older, except now they sought it from the tall, sweating bottles that were delivered to the house each morning at an ungodly hour. The boys, especially, knocked back glass after glass of milk. They shot up quickly, both of them athletic and full of muscle. Edward, the baby of the family, seemed the most soulful of the three children. Once, when he was four years old, he had asked her, "Does love have a color?"

"What do you mean, Edward?" she said, startled by his question.

"You know, when you think of love, do you see a color?"

Claire nodded. "Green," she said simply,

for she was picturing the grass all around the gazebo, how lush and green it was every year on May 27 when she met Martin there. They had not missed a single anniversary, not even during these childbearing years. Daniel continued to be unhappy about the meetings at the gazebo, but he didn't try and stop her, or make her change her mind. "I mean, I can't forbid you," he said. "And if it's the thing that for some reason keeps everything else afloat—then I suppose I shouldn't complain."

"Thank you," Claire had said quietly. Daniel didn't understand—how could he?—but he accepted it anyway. He made sure to be busy on that particular day at dusk, to be nowhere near the town square, for he didn't want to see her there with this man who had a hold over her. Slowly, Daniel grew used to the inevitability of this day. And the entire town grew used to it, too, to the sight of Martin and Claire sitting together in the gazebo once a year—right out there in plain sight. The gossiping ceased.

She had come to the gazebo eight months pregnant with Edward one May 27, and although Martin had heard that Claire was going to have another baby—his old notary public friend, Hush, continued to write him—he seemed shocked by her appearance.

"Look at you," Martin kept repeating. "God, look at you."

"You're making me self-conscious," Claire said, but secretly she was pleased by his reaction. She enjoyed being pregnant, feeling her body expand and change. It was like having a secret that she shared with everyone—a paradox that didn't exactly make sense, but there it was. Her breasts were heavier, her pale skin was flushed all the time, and her hair was somehow more textured. Her stomach swelled outward and her navel had popped, a fact that embarrassed her a little. There was a fine vertical tracing of golden hair down the center of her abdomen. Sometimes Claire stood before the mirror and looked at herself, amazed at what was happening inside her.

"Can I touch?" Martin asked. She nodded, and as they sat beside each other in the gazebo he reached out and placed one of his hands on her stomach. "Oh," he said when his hand met the swell of skin, and she knew he longed to kiss her, to cover her with his hands, his mouth, to be buried again in her hair and her citrus scent, but he did not move his hand at all from its station on her stomach. This hand had touched her so many hundreds of times before, had explored everywhere, the fingers splayed, inquisitive, but now they were respectful and almost shy, for this was someone else's territory and not his own. His eyes closed and he breathed in hard, as if trying to steady himself. Beneath the skin was someone else's baby, the tiny brine-shrimp-size creature blossoming, sprouting hands, becoming human, his mother's child, and his father's.

Martin kept his hand cupped on the curve of her stomach, and just then the baby kicked. He was shocked, pulling his hand away for a second as though he had touched a hot stove. "It moved!" Martin said, smiling, but revealing something else, a sadness beyond words, a brief, ecstatic flare followed by a great letdown. Although they tried and tried, Frances was unable to conceive more children, and this was a source of mute, lasting sadness between her and Martin. He had never before felt a shiver of life under his hand. Claire knew that he had sometimes fantasized about one day placing a hand over her stomach, as he had just done, feeling the baby move and swim and flutter deep inside her. But the baby, in all these fantasies, was his.

In 1965 Martin and Frances's fifteen-year-old daughter, Louisa, who had become an expert equestrienne, was thrown from the horse she was riding in Hampstead Heath, and severed three vertebrae in her back. At first the doctors said her situation was very grave and that she might never have the use of her legs again, but Frances and Louisa moved to the countryside for six months so that Louisa could stay at a rehabilitation clinic there, and very slowly she learned to walk. It was a traumatic time for all of them, and though Martin was there every weekend and on the phone to her every day, Frances complained that Martin cared more about the restaurant than he did about her and the child.

"That's not true," he said patiently, but he understood what she was getting at. He would easily have thrown over the restaurant for his family—that wasn't even a question—but the restaurant would always have a hold on him. When he was at work in the huge, bright, industrial kitchen, which he had tailored over the years to suit his needs exactly, he entered an almost meditative state. The rest of the world fell away from him, the memory that there was a big roomful of hungry people sitting at linen-covered tables nearby, waiting for their grilled snapper or their cheese plates, or that he had a daughter who had been seriously injured and a beautiful, stately wife who was very frightened about it, and who sometimes seemed inconsolable. Instead, he thought only about the chopping, the peeling, the stirring, the combining. His hands moved very fast, as Nicole had taught him long ago at the kitchen counter in his parents' house, and he worked himself into a trance. While he cooked, he sometimes daydreamed about Claire, picturing her when she was young and unencumbered and still belonged to him. Sometimes he got lost in these thoughts, entering into them completely, almost imagining that Claire was still that optimistic, hatless girl, and that he was that arrogant and passionate boy who loved her.

Late at night, when the restaurant was finally closing, the waiters gone home for the night, the lights extinguished in the cool, dim, gazebolike dining room, where the tables were already laid for tomorrow's lunch, the heavy silver gleaming faintly and the water glasses shining, Martin left through the front door, walking out onto the cobblestones of Dobson Mews and heading toward his own home in Bloomsbury, empty now that Frances and Louisa had gone to live for a while in the country. The first thing he would think, when he walked into his sweeping living room with its rows of books and soft white couches and throw rugs, was how different this place was from the flat above the restaurant, where he had planned to continue living with Claire. Upon Martin's marriage, though, he had moved out of the flat and into the many rooms of Frances's house. He liked it when he and Frances were there together. Frances was a decent, gentle, responsible woman, and he had a certain ease with her. They played duets on the piano, they read to each other, they went to the theater, they rubbed each other's shoulders sometimes at the end of the day. They took shared pride in Louisa's intelligence and grace, and they had developed a circle of good friends, other couples with similar interests and lives.

In the bedroom he sat on the edge of the

high bed and slowly removed his clothes, letting his shoes and pants drop to the floor, the belt buckle clanking, realizing that his body felt different than it used to—somehow a little slower, less forceful as it moved though the world. His black hair now had the occasional silver in it—not much, just a bit, giving him a distinguished look appropriate for a chef, but what that silver signified was undeniable. He had been aware of Claire getting older each year, but now he began to understand that he was getting older, too, and that his body would continue its uphill climb, and the silver would thicken and multiply, and the years would pass and he still wouldn't have her.

Lucas Swift died of a stroke in his home in 1966, with his daughter Claire sitting in a chair beside him, holding his hand. He had suffered a smaller stroke a few weeks earlier and had refused to be taken to the hospital in Albany. "NO POINT" he had written in a ragged hand on a tablet of paper, for his speech had become confused. So he stayed at home, and Claire helped him exercise each day, wrapping his fingers around a pliant rubber ball and making him squeeze, and trying to get him to sit up in bed for a few moments each day. But the will wasn't there. His wife, Maureen, was long gone, and now he saw that he would have a chance to follow her, so there was really no reason to fight this thing that had left him with a mouth twisted into a perennial half frown, one hand like a claw and a mind like a forgetful child's. He would stay at home for the remainder of his life.

That remainder proved short, for another stroke came a few weeks later, and Claire moved in with her father once again. Daniel took care of the children and fixed them dinner. Though he wasn't a good cook, he could prepare a simple stew. Claire sat holding her father's tight hand, stroking his arm and talking to him about the past. When he died, she thought that she had done what her mother had asked her to do, and now her job was through. Swift Maintenance was on solid footing, too, having expanded its reach and rented part of a spacious warehouse nearby to store all its tools and parts and house its offices. Now, Claire thought with some measure of irony, she was ready to leave Longwood Falls and join Martin across the ocean. But life was sometimes like an elaborate game of jump rope, which she used to play for hours with her friends on the bumpy sidewalks of Badger Street; if you didn't jump in at the right moment, you could never jump in at all.

When the undertaker with the nervous blinking tic from Barker's Funeral Home came, Claire kissed her father's hand. "I love you," she said to him softly, and then she stood, heading home to her husband and children, who were waiting.

On May 26, 1968, Martin walked through the streets of London, looking for a taxi to take him to the airport. London had completely changed since he had first moved here in the 1950s; it was now filled with teenagers, music, and overly bright colors and an array of drugs, none of which interested him particularly, and all of which his daughter, Louisa, loved. She was a brilliant girl who wore miniskirts made out of paper, spent her time with stupid boys on motorbikes, incessantly played the same rock songs, and applied so much black kohl makeup around her eyes that she looked like a sick raccoon. Still, he couldn't blame her, for she'd had a long recovery from her riding accident, and now she was well again, so she had chosen to go out into the world and embrace all of it.

It wasn't that Martin was stodgy; just last week, John Lennon and Paul McCartney and a couple of music executives had come to dinner at the Gazebo, and Martin had felt thrilled, peeking out through the round glass window of the kitchen door throughout the meal. To his immense pleasure, both Beatles finished every bit of food on their plates. He thought to himself, *I must tell Claire,* for he would be seeing her very soon.

Although Martin took comfort from his wife and daughter, and from his professional success, and although he'd been the subject of various newspaper and magazine articles and was about to publish a cookbook called *Recipes from the Gazebo*, he often felt as though he were living a dream life. It was as though his sleeping self was here in England while his active, waking self was off exploring a narrow street in Italy with Claire.

Frances tolerated Martin's annual visits to Longwood Falls, though she never liked them. While she knew they were "innocent," she was still threatened, and she had a right to be. He loved seeing Claire; it was the mo-

ment in each year that still made him hap-
piest, that made him truly alive. Would he
be this happy if they were together all the
time? It was hard to say. Frances always
complained a bit before he left, sitting before
her vanity mirror in the big bedroom and lifting her heavy hair off her neck (she had
graduated from the long braid of her earlier
years to a more elegant chignon), and saying, "Is she much more beautiful than I am?
Is that it?"

"No," he would say as he packed his
briefcase and his overnight bag. "She's not.
Not at all."

"Then she's smarter," Frances would say.

"She doesn't even have a college education," Martin would reply. "And you got a
first in philosophy at Cambridge."

Frances snorted lightly. "A lot of good it
does me," she said. "I hardly get much of a
chance to be a philosopher shopping in Har-
rods."

"But you chose your life," he said.

Frances looked in the mirror and their
eyes caught. "Yes," she said. "You chose
your life, too, Martin."

"I'm fully aware of that," he replied.

"Aren't I a good husband? Don't we have a nice time of it?"

"Yes," she admitted. "We do." And it was true; they did.

"All I want is once a year to be allowed to go off quietly like this," he said. "I don't really think it's so much to ask for, and yet you always make a fuss."

"I'm sorry, darling," Frances said, and then she suddenly stood and turned around to him, kissing him full on the mouth and taking him by surprise. Her kisses were always intense and deeply felt and absorbing. Out of the corner of his eye he could see the embrace in the vanity mirror. He stopped packing his clothes and kissed her in return, for he was her husband, and he did, after all, love her.

A day later, he was back in Longwood Falls, stepping off the platform into another warm afternoon. The world had changed so much in the 1960s, but the changes hadn't seemed to affect this little corner of it. There was still a sleepiness here, a leisurely quality. The primary feeling Martin had when he entered the square was: *this is the town where Claire lives.* That thought was foremost in his mind, stronger than the thought that this was the town where he himself had grown up. His childhood was rapidly fading, the memories of the big white house with the slippery floors starting to dim.

But as he walked along the path toward the gazebo—half an hour early today, and Claire was not yet there—his childhood suddenly came barreling back to him. For his father and mother were walking toward him on the path. There was no way he could avoid them; although they had not yet seen him, they were coming straight at him, and he felt his heart begin to race. He had put aside most thoughts of his parents over the years, although sometimes he dreamed about them. Did they dream about him, or think about him at all? They had never tried to contact him, their only son, though even if they had, he didn't know what he would have done. Now here they were, the mother and father he had not seen in fifteen years, and he was shocked.

First of all, his mother had grown fat; though she had once been slender and blonde, drinking had coarsened her, as it inevitably does to everyone who dedicates a life to it. Her eyes seemed to be swimming, and her walk was unsteady, not because she was drunk, but merely because her metabolism had been thrown off balance. She was wearing a hat, of course, this one the color of a beet and sitting flat on her head, as though it had landed there from another planet.

But the more surprising change was in his father, who had lost his luster, his overt rage. He seemed like a weak man who was growing old. He was still probably a mean man, uncharitable and full of a desire for revenge against various perceived enemies, but the anger that had once driven him was buried inside an old man's face. His hair, which had been thick and dark like Martin's, was thin. It wasn't threaded through with silver, as was his son's, but instead was a watery gray, the color of age. His skin seemed mottled, and he walked slowly. No one would feel threatened by such a man, Martin thought, and he couldn't believe that he had spent so much of his childhood in fear of his father.

Now they saw him. It happened all at once. Lucinda Rayfiel gasped, squeezed her husband's upper arm, and said, "Look."

They stopped on the path about six feet from one another. The parents regarded their child, and he met their gaze. "Mother," Martin said. Then, nodding, he added, "Father."

"Oh, Martin," said his mother, and she burst forward and pressed herself against him. "What are you doing here?" she asked him.

"I'm here to see a friend," he answered, his voice careful.

"Oh? A good friend?" asked his mother.

"Yes. Very good."

"Look at you," his mother went on. "All grown up and so distinguished." He put an arm around her, patting her on the back, as if consoling a child. And like a child she sobbed against him, as though realizing in this moment all that she had missed out on over the years that they had not spoken. Throughout her tears, Ash Rayfiel appeared embarrassed, his hands shoved in his pockets, looking away from this display of emotion. Martin was partly moved, partly not. He felt no desire to cry, but he did feel genuine regret at the loss of a mother. Of course, she had been lost to him long before he had ever gone off to Europe.

Claire, on the other hand, was a good mother; he knew this from his friend Hush, who was still dutifully sending Martin periodic reports. Hush, who now had a child of his own, a few years younger than Claire's children, had said that Claire was a devoted, indefatigable mother, always creating wild Halloween costumes for her children and attending every performance of the school concerts they were in, listening proudly to each squeak of their clarinets, and always available to help them memorize lines of a play or prepare a science project involving lima beans and cotton balls. She was available to them; she was *there.* If Martin and Claire had had children together, as they had so much wanted, she would have been there.

Martin's mother pulled back now, and he saw that she had an apologetic look on her face; it was apparent in her swimmy eyes and on the cheeks that were a shade too red from both rouge and broken capillaries. "Oh, Martin," she said. "I wish we could start again."

"Me, too," he said.

"You're doing well, we hear," Lucinda Rayfiel said. "We have friends in London; you remember the Babbingtons from the club—Bill and Norma?"

He nodded, though he had no idea who they were.

"Well, they moved to London some years ago, and they often write to us and say what a big shot you are," she went on. "Once they even sent us a newspaper clipping from the London *Times* about you! We're terribly proud, of course, and we wanted to tell you that, but your father thought it best—" Her voice broke off here; she looked away.

Now Ash gazed directly at Martin, his eyes as impassive as ever, and stiffly said, "I thought it best to leave you to your way of life. Not to interfere. You never liked interference."

"That's right, I never did," Martin replied, but he knew that it wasn't courtesy that had kept his father away; it was strong dislike, almost hatred. You couldn't really see it in Ash Rayfiel's stance, for he was really just an aging, fading man in expensive clothes, but Martin knew it was there, blazing somewhere beneath the surface.

"Will you come up to the house?" his mother asked. "Alex has the car waiting around the corner."

"What happened to Henry?" Martin

asked, remembering the kind chauffeur he used to sit beside in the Bentley.

"Oh, Henry died years ago," said his mother. "A brain tumor. It was very sad, really."

"I'm sorry to hear that," Martin said. He wished he had known; he would have attended the funeral and visited Henry's wife, who worked as a housekeeper elsewhere in the Crest. Henry was dead, and so was the large Swiss cook who had an obsession with cheese, not to mention an aunt and two uncles. "I can't come to the house, Mother, I'm sorry," Martin went on. "I have to see my friend now. But maybe you could visit me in London sometime. I know you and Father like to travel."

"Thank you, Martin," she said. "We actually don't travel much anymore, but perhaps we'll come." He kissed her good-bye, and his father nodded briskly, and then they were off, slowly continuing their stroll across the center of the square. He knew they would never come to visit him in London; he knew that there was a good chance he might never see them again.

Martin sat in the gazebo, shocked and recovering. In a while Claire joined him. Her pale hair was cut shorter around her face, and her arms looked long and graceful against the vanilla-colored blouse she wore. There was a string of bright beads around her neck: a gift from her daughter, Alison, she said.

"You still smell exactly the same," he said into her neck. She drew back and smiled at him. Across the lawn, a man stood staring at the two of them. Occasionally someone did this—gawked briefly at Martin and Claire, the platonic couple who still met every year, but no one ever interrupted them, or said anything. Claire's children seemed to know nothing about Martin.

"Do you know how hard it is to find this citrus soap?" Claire said to Martin. "I have to search everywhere in the entire area for it. Spicer's Drugstore stopped carrying it, and now I have to drive to Albany. But I know how much you like it."

"I do," he said. "Thank you for driving to Albany." As they sat together, she told him of her life over the past year, some of which he already knew about through Hush's letters but which he pretended he was learning for the first time. "Are you sculpting at all?" he asked her.

"Sometimes," she said evasively; she was always evasive when he asked about her sculpting. Perhaps it embarrassed her to be reminded of this talent that she had not been able to see to fruition. He feared she wasn't sculpting at all, but that she didn't want to tell him that. He didn't pursue it.

"How's the Gazebo?" she asked. "The one that serves food, I mean."

He was about to launch into some stories from the life of the restaurant, and to tell her about the upcoming cookbook, but he couldn't bear it. That was just small talk. He saw her so infrequently, and for such a brief period of time, that the idea of making small talk with her was unthinkable. "Claire," he suddenly said, "let's not speak to each other like strangers sitting together on a train who are making polite conversation. Please," he added.

She nodded. "All right," she said.

He looked hard at her for a long moment. "Do you remember the first time we went to the Lookout?" he asked.

She smiled, both shy and ironic, and said, "You made me impure that day."

Martin shook his head. "You're not even

impure *now*. I don't know what the word means."

Claire looked down at the floor of the gazebo, struggling to say something. "That day," she said. "It changed my life."

Even though she had ended up back in the same town where she was born, married to a man from the area and helping to run her father's business—in essence, leading a life of quiet, even predictability, like the lives of many other people she knew—she felt that her life had been changed that day. It had not all been for nothing. Sometimes he worried that she thought it had, that what they had briefly lived out together had been pointless. "So you're not sorry?" he said. "About that day, and what happened after?"

Claire looked at him strangely. "Martin," she said, "I can't believe you'd think I was sorry."

"I'm so glad to hear that," he said, and he held her hands for a while, until she had to get back home.

In 1975 Claire's oldest child, Alison Martina Clusker, a champion runner on the Longwood Falls High track team and extremely talented at drawing, was accepted to art school in New York on a substantial scholarship. For Claire, who hadn't had a chance to study art so intensively herself, this was a thrill. Whenever she came upon Alison standing at an easel she had set up in the cluttered attic of their small house, she would feel moved by all the possibilities that were in store for her daughter. Alison had a boyfriend already, a brooding boy named Jeff who worked after school at Beckerman's soda shop, serving soft ice cream that swirled out of a nozzle. Claire tried to stay out of Alison and Jeff's way, allowing them to sit in the front seat of the family car for hours late at night doing God knows what. But lately Alison seemed unhappy, sometimes bursting into tears at the dinner table for no obvious reason and pushing away her plate of food and flinging herself from the room.

"Teenage girls," Daniel commented mildly. "I feel for her. But they all go through this, don't they? Isn't it a rite of passage?"

"I guess," said Claire, but she was worried. One night after Alison left the table in tears for the second time that week, Claire knocked on her daughter's door and asked to come in. At first there was no reply, and then finally Alison opened the door, her face streaky and pink from crying. "What?" she said miserably to her mother. Behind her was her poster-filled room with its clutter of candles, paperback books, paintbrushes, makeup, and hills of clothes. Draped over the back of a chair was Claire's old apple-green Chanel suit, which she had given her daughter, for it no longer fit her. Alison liked wearing the suit, calling it "vintage," and a "throwback," and usually putting on a pair of Swedish clogs with it, and some interesting jewelry that she made in art class at school out of copper wire and beads.

"I just wanted to make sure you're okay, honey," said Claire. "If there's anything you'd like to talk about, I'd be—"

"Mom," interrupted Alison, "there's nothing here that I could talk about with you. I mean, just look at you and Dad. You obviously haven't experienced anything close to what I'm going through."

"Oh no?" said Claire.

"No," said her daughter. "What I'm going through is about . . . love. About feeling things so much you feel all crazy inside. No offense, but it's not something you could ever understand."

It was all Claire could do to keep from coming into the room, shutting the door hard behind her, sitting Alison down on the bed, and saying, "Look, you, I know *exactly* what you're talking about. Your mom has led a secret life of love and passion that would shock you out of your skin." Her daughter would have been incredulous. For how could this middle-aged mother of three—this average, mild, small-town woman—have had such passions? Sometimes Claire herself wondered.

So all she did now was give her daughter a sympathetic look and say, "Well, if you ever want to try me, I'm here." And then she left the room, knowing that within moments Alison would be on the telephone to Jeff, whispering and crying and laughing and murmuring things that no one else would ever hear.

When Martin's mother died in 1987 of pancreatitis, a result of chronic alcoholism, Hush called him, and he came back for the funeral, sitting with his back straight in the church. He'd imagined that there would be whispers about his return, but then he realized that most of those people who would have done the whispering were probably dead. Two years later, when Ash Rayfiel died of an aneurysm in his office at the hat factory, Martin did not return. The funeral, it was reported, was only sparsely attended. The house on the Crest was sold, and all the Rayfiel money went to Princeton University, where a new building of some sort was supposed to be named in Ash Rayfiel's memory. Martin didn't care; he hadn't expected any money. He was a very wealthy man on his own now, someone who had gathered money and great success and worked at a job he truly loved, and had a wide circle of friends in London and throughout the Continent. Every month or so he and Frances invited their friends to the restaurant, and they all had dinner at one round table and stayed up very late laughing, eating big plates of food, leaning back in their chairs and glancing up at the soaring ceiling of the restaurant.

His wife and daughter were flourishing. Frances did volunteer work giving tours at the British Museum, and Louisa, who had attended Cambridge, was now, amazingly, a philosophy don there, as her late father, James, had been. She'd long ago abandoned her paper skirts and raccoon makeup for a more serious though still stylish wardrobe.

Martin's hair went entirely silver by the time he turned fifty-five. When he showed up at the gazebo that year, Claire's eyes widened. He hadn't realized how extreme the change in his own appearance had been since the year before. "Do I look very old?" he asked her.

"Oh no," she said. "You just look important. Which you always were, of course. Only now you've grown into it."

"Thank you," he said. He held her hand and lightly stroked her arm, which bore a spattering of freckles he hadn't noticed before. Age spots, he thought, but they didn't bother him; they just provided a map to Claire at fifty-five, this beautiful woman who was human and was aging like everyone else. He loved what was imperfect about her; he loved what was real. "You know," he said softly, "nothing makes me happier than coming here."

"Oh, me too," she said.

"It's funny," he said. "We both have these lives, you know? You've got your children, and Daniel, and Swift Maintenance. And I've got the other Gazebo—capital *G*—and my wife and Louisa the philosopher, and yet when we come here, it's as though everything else is of no concern."

"That's right," she said. "It's exactly like that for me, too."

They sat and leaned into each other, their hands entwined, not caring who was watching them. Their story was old news by now. He told Claire a good recipe for cold tomato soup with dill, and she brought his hand to her mouth and kissed the fingertips, one by one.

They both imagined that it would go on like this indefinitely: meeting once a year, sitting and talking and holding hands, letting each other know that the love was still lingering like a scent, and that it would never go away. But on May 27, 1998, when she was sixty-six years old, Claire was very somber as Martin slowly walked up the steps of the gazebo and sat down beside her.

"What is it?" he asked, frightened, but in his heart he must have known.

She too was afraid; she didn't know how to tell him. She had been dreading it much more than telling Daniel or her children. At least the Cluskers were a family, and a close one; at least they could all cope with it together. But Martin had no one around him in London he could talk to about this, or with whom he could cry freely. "Martin," she began, "now listen to me." And she began to tell him what had happened.

Ten weeks earlier, Claire and Daniel had been getting ready for sleep. He sat on his side of the bed pulling on his pajama top, and Claire sat on her side of the bed applying moisturizer to her face and buttoning her nightgown. She and Daniel had an ease to their marriage; it had only increased as the years passed, and she felt devotion toward this shy, hardworking man who still, even at the age of sixty-six, did the occasional handspring, as he had done when he was young. He had been a calm and steady husband and a good father to their three children, who were all grown now and with families of their own. Serious Jonathan lived in Northern California with his wife and daughter and designed computer software; soulful Edward and his wife, both cellists, lived in Boston with their two sons, where they performed with the symphony orchestra. And Alison Martina Clusker, who had kept her maiden name, had married her high school sweetheart, Jeff, and the couple lived in Vermont with their three children—two girls and a boy—where she was an artist and he taught school. Grandchildren were everywhere in Claire and Daniel's life, coming to visit for Christmas or summer vacations. She doted on these children and had knitted each one a beautiful scarf last winter, using an entire rainbow of wool.

As Claire sat on the side of the bed that night before sleep, she raised one arm over her head and lightly began touching her breast, as she did every month, checking to make sure nothing was there that shouldn't be there. Usually she spent just a few casual moments on this task, but tonight something made her pause. It was tiny, no bigger than a pearl; had she imagined it? She palpated the left breast again with a little more urgency.

"Daniel," she whispered. "I think I found something."

The surgery was only marginally successful; the doctors said that the cancer had spread to the lymph glands under her arm. When she woke up in the hospital in Albany, she took one look at her husband's face and knew. She had only one breast now, a fact that saddened her. Daniel said it didn't matter, all that mattered was that she was okay, but she had the strong sense that she wasn't okay.

A round of chemotherapy had left her weakened. She lost weight, and when she looked at herself in the mirror in the morning she barely recognized herself. Oddly, she looked younger than she had in a long time, more like a fragile girl than the old, sick woman of sixty-six that she really was. The cancer was still circulating in her body—the same type of cancer that had caused her mother to die forty-four years earlier. She remembered her mother's suffering; she thought about it often now, the way Maureen Swift's eyes had glazed over and she had turned her head away in pain, not wanting Claire to see.

Oh, Mother, Claire thought, *here I am, a woman in her sixties, someone you'll never meet, and I'm going through exactly what you went through. Tell me what I should do.* But of course her mother couldn't reach across time and space to answer. Claire had only herself to figure it out. The chemotherapy was so harsh, and the chances were not good anyway, and so she had decided: enough. She would have no more.

Claire explained her decision to Daniel, and he wept and asked her to reconsider. She held his head as he cried, and she assured him that it was the right decision, and that though it would be hard, he would be okay without her. He had children and grandchildren and a townful of friends. "We've loved each other," she told him.

"Yes," Daniel said, "we have. And we do."

Her illness was a difficult subject to talk about with her husband and her children, yet she had done it. But telling Martin—now this was a different thing entirely. At the gazebo after the surgery and the chemotherapy and the decision not to proceed with treatment, Claire faced Martin and spoke for a while. As she talked, he sat and listened, his face crumpling slightly from time to time. When she was finished, he didn't respond for a moment. There was a protracted pause, and then Martin took a deep breath and knelt down before her.

"I want you to know," he said slowly, "that you're still my love." His voice was halting. His hair was entirely silver, and here she was discussing *her* illness, *her* death, but all she could think of was how amazing and how sad it was that he was old now, too—this man whose hair had once been black and whose face and body had been boyish, lean, hopeful. "You're still my love," he continued, "and whatever you do, you'll know that I'm right there. And even if you're afraid—" Here Martin's voice broke off. He put his face in his hands for a moment, and she watched as his shoulders shook. Then he calmed himself and looked up again. "There won't be one moment where I'm not with you," he said. He held her hand tightly. "Just think of my hand in yours," he went on. "And the way it was when we were together. Just you and me, completely in love. Think of all those hotel beds in Europe, and those dinners, and those long walks. Kissing in front of every monument. We couldn't get enough of each other."

"No, we couldn't," she said, and she was crying now, too.

"It won't end," he said. "This won't stop with death; how could it? I'll always think of you, my love. And before I go, too, I'll find some way that what we had—our time together—gets remembered. That it stays on this earth."

They leaned into each other and sobbed openly, wildly, kissing each other, feeling their faces grow slick with tears, arms wrapping hard around each other. "I love you, Martin," she said to him. "And I've loved you since the first moment we saw each other right here in this very place."

"With my swollen eye," he said.

"And with my peach-colored dress," she said. She paused. "What happened to those two people?" she asked him, thinking back over the decades—the enormous span of years they had spent both together and apart.

Martin paused. "They haven't gone anywhere," he said softly. "They're right here."

The church was packed. So many people came to Claire's funeral in July that it was standing room only. Martin had heard of her death through Hush, and numbly he had flown in for the funeral, entering at the last minute and standing in the back so her husband would not see him, though even if he had, Martin didn't know if Daniel would know it was him. Various people stood and said a few words at the podium, eloquently speaking about this ordinary yet extraordinary woman who had been born and raised and had died in Longwood Falls. He saw her children—her two strong, handsome sons and her beautiful daughter, Alison, who resembled Claire so much that Martin was startled.

When Alison stood and began to speak, Martin held his breath for a moment. Her voice was just like Claire's, though trembling and on the verge of tears. Claire's daughter was already much older than Claire herself had been when he'd fallen in love with her.

"My mother," Alison began, as she stood at the podium, "was an average person. Occasionally she would take a quiz in a women's magazine: 'How Perceptive Are You?' 'How Wild Are You?' And her score would be . . . average. It always drove her a little crazy." There was light laughter in the church. Alison smiled slightly, wiping at her tears with a handkerchief. "Of course," she went on, "those of us who knew my mother well are aware that this 'average' business is ridiculous. Because who in this room is average? Who doesn't have something that no one else has? Who isn't an original?" Alison looked out over the congregation. "Like everyone here, my mom was an original. She used to design these incredible Halloween costumes for my brothers and me. One year, Eddie went door to door in the neighorhood dressed as Michelangelo's statue *David*—with a fig leaf, in case you were wondering." More laughter. "I suppose she was a frustrated artist," said Alison. "But she never seemed frustrated to us kids. She seemed overwhelmed, and harried, and funny, and amazingly patient. Other mothers always seemed a little overprotective to me, but Mom let us be kind of . . . free. And I'll always be grateful for that." Alison paused, the tears streaming down her face now. "Mom," she said, "I'm sorry I was such a pain in the neck during adolescence. And I'm sorry that I didn't always realize how much you had to offer everyone. Because I see that it isn't just about what a person does in her life—some résumé or list of incredible achievements—or even about whether a person gets to live in some perfect way that they'd always dreamed of. It's about whether or not you chose to put yourself out there so that other people could join you. Whether you were *generous* with yourself. And, as all of you know, my mom was. And I'm so, so sorry for all the years that I was too ignorant to see that." Alison stopped, taking a long breath, then she composed herself and continued. "And I'm especially thankful for these last few years, when I saw what my mom had to give, and I took some of it. As all of you here have taken some of it, too. She wanted that, she really did. Okay, so she wasn't world famous, she wasn't absolutely brilliant, she wasn't out there in the 'great big world,' wherever that is. But she was in *this* world—our world. And we were all so lucky to be there with her."

When Alison was done speaking, she quietly sat down beside her father and brothers, who reached out to embrace her. It seemed to Martin that there were endless tears at the funeral; they just went on and on. Eventually Claire's casket was strewn with wildflowers, and then there were hymns, the entire congregation singing out as if in one voice.

Martin felt that he might fall over now in a faint, but he steadied himself against the church wall, listening to the music and letting the tears flood his face and stream down onto his shirt. *I am with you,* he told her silently, as he had promised. *I am right there by your side. And I will never, ever forget any of it—who we were, what we did, and how we were two people who loved each other over time in the best way that we knew how.*

When the service was over, someone threw open the double doors, letting in the day. And it was at that moment that Daniel Clusker stood and looked directly at Martin, and Martin looked back. After a moment, Daniel nodded, acknowledging Martin's presence, yet not saying a word. There was no anger there, no jealousy, just a silent acceptance between two men who had loved the same woman. After a few seconds, Daniel turned away, and someone embraced him. All around the room, people stood and embraced one another, unwilling to leave just yet, wanting to stay just a little bit more in the cool of the church and the hovering memory of this wonderful woman who was gone. But Martin Rayfiel could not stay. Before anyone else noticed he was there, he hurried out into the sunlight with Claire beside him, her hand in his.

CHAPTER ELEVEN

The last tape was over. Martin seemed to sigh as he spoke the words at the very end, and then there was nothing, just silence. Abby reached over to shut off the cassette player, and then all she could do was gaze blankly out the window for a moment, where another dawn was rising over the square.

She was tired and terribly sad and lost in the story of all she had heard. But on her desk, Martin's briefcase was still open on its brass hinges, and Abby could see that there were a few other items left inside: a recipe from Martin's new cookbook, an announcement of a philosophy lecture his daughter had given at Cambridge, and, finally, a folded piece of paper of some sort. She opened it. It was a document, and at the top she read: APPLICATION FOR U.S. PASSPORT. CLAIRE SWIFT. MAY 28, 1952.

So this was the paper that Claire had gotten notarized without a birth certificate all those years ago. Abby started to set it aside, on top of the pile of items she had removed from the briefcase over the course of the long night, but then she thought: Why was it here, at the bottom of the briefcase? All the other items had been in roughly chronological order, from the receipts at the Lookout Motel all the way through various announcements of the births of Claire's grandchildren. Martin had been so methodical in the way he'd arranged everything; this oversight didn't seem like him at all.

Abby studied the page more closely now. She read the details of the application, the information about her life that Claire had needed to provide, but everything seemed in order: date of birth, the address on Badger, the names of her father and mother. Abby read it all again, thinking she'd missed something, going over every word right down to the bottom of the page and the seal of the notary public nicknamed Hush, a man who had taken a personal risk and helped Claire get a passport, all because he believed in giving love precedence over all else. Abby examined the seal, running her finger along the raised bumps.

And then she saw it. Beneath the seal was a signature, the full name of the man Martin had called Hush.

"Thomas Reston," Abby read, and her hand immediately flew to her mouth. The notary public was Abby's father.

All those years ago, her very own father had been so much in love that he had done a favor for another young couple. Abby couldn't believe it; she had always thought of him as an unemotional man, and while her mother had tried to say that wasn't true at all, Abby hadn't been convinced. "Hush"— Tom Reston—had been wildly in love with a woman—Abby's mother. So they hadn't had a slightly dull, no-nonsense marriage; they had had passion, and overwhelming sensations and experiences that their daughter couldn't begin to know about. But they *had* had them; that much she now knew. It was true that he was taciturn— hushed was the word—but he was more than that. He was more complex than Abby had ever fully been able to grasp, and the way he'd loved her mother, Helen—even the way he'd loved Abby—had been private, quiet, but *felt.*

No wonder Martin had chosen Abby to tell everything to; no wonder he had insisted that she was the only one to whom he wanted to leave these belongings and this entire story. It was as though Abby and her father had shared an old friend and hadn't known it.

Abby got up and started gathering the papers she'd spent the night removing from the briefcase. She tried to put them back the way she'd found them, even honoring Martin Rayfiel's decision to leave the passport application at the bottom, but when she picked up the first pile to place it back in the briefcase she saw that one last thing remained. It was a small envelope, and it was addressed to Martin, in a handwriting that looked like Claire's, though it was shaky, spidery, clearly written at the end of her life. It had been opened, and inside it, she saw, was a key.

Abby picked it up. The key was attached to a beaded metal chain with a tag on it that said SWIFT MAINTENANCE, STORAGE ROOM B. She held it in her hand, weighing it, just as several hours earlier she'd hefted the stack of cassette tapes. *Don't ask the question unless you want to know the answer.*

And then Abby slipped the key in her pocket. Why not? she thought. After all, she'd come this far.

Trembling slightly—whether from exhaustion or emotion, she wasn't sure—Abby put the papers back in the briefcase and carefully closed it, shut off her desk lamp, and stood. She walked down the hall lined with framed front pages of the *Ledger,* but she didn't leave the newspaper's offices yet. Before she headed across the square and down a few streets to the offices of Swift Maintenance, there was still one more thing she needed to see here.

She stopped at the room called the library, which housed all the old editions of the newspaper, volume upon volume bound in green binding with gold embossed letters on the spines, since the paper had been founded in 1846. Abby climbed a rolling ladder and reached for the volume marked "July–December, 1998." Flipping quickly through the pages, she found what she was looking for:

Clusker, Claire, age 66, died in her home yesterday after a brave battle with cancer. Married to Daniel Clusker and mother of three children, Alison, Jonathan, and Edward, Mrs. Clusker was born and raised in Longwood Falls. Survivors include her husband, children, and six grandchildren, as well as a sister, Mrs. Margaret Benton, also of Longwood Falls.

Mrs. Clusker. Abby shook her head slightly, and read on:

Devlin, Randall, age 38, died in Schenectady Regional Hospital on Friday from injuries sustained in a car accident. He is survived by his mother, Ruth Devlin, of Albany, and by one brother, Matthew Devlin, of Pensacola, Florida.

Abby flipped to the next day's edition of the *Ledger*. There she read:

Cushing, Sandra, age 82, died of a
stroke on Saturday . . .

Below that came "Starrett, Harold," and
then, the following day, "Bradford, Norman,"
"McLoughlin, Jenny," "Michaels, Louis."
The day following that brought "Kibbing,
Mark," "Lomax, Edgar," "Santino, John,"
and then Abby slammed the volume shut.

She stepped back and looked up at the
wall of volumes in the library. Here lay the
lives and deaths of Longwood Falls, neatly
ordered and bound in leather.

All of it was true, and all of it was wrong.

Abby closed the door of the library,
walked down the silent hallway, and then
opened the front door of the *Ledger* offices,
heading outside into the dawn. It was May
28 now, she realized, and it seemed to her
like the first day of a new year. The town
square was completely still, the grass wet,
the gazebo shimmering. She walked right
past it and headed down a sloping street,
passing all the houses with the shades still
drawn, people asleep in warm beds, or else
getting up and standing at basins and starting their day. Nobody knew what really went
on in anyone else's house—or in anyone

else's life, for that matter. Claire *had* been those things that had been written about her in her obituary, but she had been more, too. In her death, Claire Swift had been known as Mrs. Claire Clusker, wife, mother, grandmother. Certainly she had been admirable in all those roles, but they didn't begin to touch on all the other details about her that had made her life unique. Abby hadn't done her father justice; her father, in his role as editor of the *Ledger* the previous summer, hadn't really done Claire justice in her obituary. He had run it, but there was so much more and he had known it but probably hadn't known what to *do* with all he knew. As Abby walked through the same streets that Claire had once walked, passing Badger Street, and Conley Street, and the grade school, and the soda shop still known as Beckerman's—as though she were going on a walking tour of Claire Swift's entire life, a tour that might have traced the life of anyone who lived in Longwood Falls—she wondered how anyone could ever begin to understand the complexities and contradictions of any other person's life.

Finally she stopped in front of the building that housed Swift Maintenance, a place she had seen for most of her life but had never noticed, just as she had never noticed this woman Claire, who had lived here the whole time Abby had been growing up, and whom she had probably passed many times in the market, or the square. Claire's children had gone to Abby's school, a few years ahead of her, and she hadn't known them either. The building, she saw now, was locked. Abby tried the key; it worked. With a squeak, the heavy steel door opened, and Abby stepped into a dim industrial hallway, feeling both anticipation and dread. She reached for a light switch; there was none. Groping along the wall, she made her way along the corridor until she reached a door. Dimly she could make out the words STORAGE ROOM A. She kept moving along the wall, and the next door she found was the right one. Again, Abby tried the key in the lock, and it, too, worked. She pushed the heavy door, and it gave, and Abby stepped from almost total darkness into almost total light.

The storage room was flooded with sun. The windows went from floor to ceiling, admitting the day. But what most astonished Abby was not the room itself but what it contained. For everywhere in this room were small, carefully crafted, beautiful sculptures: a lifetime's worth, Abby thought to herself.

Abby slowly circled the room, examining small figures that she recognized from Martin's descriptions of them on the tapes, of Martin as a young man, and the one Claire had done from memory of herself as a girl reading a book. There were long-ago sculptures of Claire's parents, Lucas and Maureen Swift, and another one of her sister, Margaret, as a teenager. But then Abby saw others that she didn't recognize, works, Abby slowly realized, that Claire couldn't have done as a girl and as a very young woman: a sculpture of Claire as a middle-aged woman, and one of her husband, Daniel, using a saw, and several of her children and grandchildren. There was a bust of Martin in later life, his face slightly weary and lined but still clearly, indisputably, the courtly, intense, elderly man who had appeared in the doorway to Abby's office two days earlier, carrying a worn briefcase.

So Claire had been working steadily all these years; yet she hadn't told Martin about it until the end of her life, when she'd sent him the key and let him find out for himself what Abby had now found out. Claire had just wanted to quietly get on with her work all those years, much of it from memory, enjoying the moments she could steal here in Storage Room B. Martin's work life had by nature been public, glorious, on display; Claire's had been private, hidden behind a plain metal door in an industrial building on the edge of town.

It occurred to Abby that she now had enough material here, enough provocative, stirring substance, to go back to her office and get started. She would translate Martin's spoken love story into something textured, a long article complete with photographs and documents and pictures of Claire's sculptures. The article would present a bit of extraordinary local history, but it would do something else, too. It would show a real life lived by two people in this town and elsewhere, something that was rarely shown, because people's lives so often were shuttered to the world. And in showing this life, Abby knew she would implicitly help Martin do what he had promised Claire he would do: find some way so that what they'd had— their time together—would be remembered. Which, she realized now, was exactly what

Martin had hoped Abby would do when he had walked into her office.

To be remembered, and to have a life worth remembering: this was what Abby wanted for herself, too. Like Claire, she thought of herself as a good, fiercely devoted mother. And her father would probably be fairly impressed at the job Abby was doing at the *Ledger*, even if he wouldn't have acknowledged it. But the area of love was still left unfinished. There was a man in New York City who had been trying to see what it might be like to love Abby. But she hadn't allowed him to see. Unlike Claire and Martin, Abby had let herself be closed to possibilities. But it was the possibilities that made one's life an astonishing story.

She wanted to be able to look back over her own life when she was much older and say: Yes, I did that. And that. And that, too. She wanted to have photographs to show for it, and letters, and papers, and an assortment of tickets and receipts and trinkets. Abby knew she would call that nice, handsome pediatrician Nick Kelleher back today; her daughter, Miranda, would be thrilled. Maybe she would take him up on his offer to drive up some weekend to see her. The

distance between New York City and Longwood Falls wasn't nearly as daunting as
New York City and London.

Now Abby thought of Martin traveling
back and forth across an ocean each year,
getting on airplanes to come be with Claire
for just a brief time. She wanted to tell Martin
how much she admired what he and Claire
had done, what they had somehow
achieved together, and what it personally
meant to Abby. But she suspected that she
wouldn't have a chance to tell him—that he
was gone.

If she knew Martin Rayfiel—and she was
beginning to think she did—he would have
left Longwood Falls by now. He would have
traveled back to London to his restaurant
and his wife and his circle of friends and
customers. What's more, she doubted he
would ever return here again. He had given
to Abby—to Hush's daughter—everything
that had belonged to him and Claire, and
now it was up to her to do with it what she
thought best.

She stood for a long time in that storage
room, so long that eventually she heard
voices nearby—people who worked at Swift
Maintenance were coming in and starting

their day, as people were surely starting to arrive at the offices of the *Ledger,* too. Right now, Kim the receptionist was probably putting on the coffeepot and humming and sporting a neon headband, and someone else was probably sliding paper into the feed tray of the copy machine.

Still Abby didn't move. She would have to go soon, but she didn't want to leave behind the world she'd discovered in Storage Room B just yet. She lingered, bending down to peer closely at sculptures. One piece she found in a corner was smaller than the others, and Abby had to pick it up in order to see what it was. The sculpture fit in her hand like a little jewel box: the gazebo. It was impossible to say how long ago Claire had made it, for the gazebo never changed from year to year, but there it was, a perfect, inviting rendering of the eight sides and the pointed roof. Abby kept looking at the sculpture in her hand until after a while she could see the two of them in there, both of them so young, Martin with his dark hair falling into his face, and Claire with her pale skin, her summer dress, her smile. They were leaning together, as they always did, and they were laughing.